BAFFLED IN BOSTON
Gary Provost

For years I had been Mr. Cool, the unflappable Jeff Scotland, the last guy you'd expect to find in Walgreen's looking for a bargain price on a large jar of Rolaids. But things had changed. And now I was the one who had to settle down, get a job, end the affair with Joan, and give up coffee, or perish.

But there was one job I wouldn't mind having, a job that would give me the fame I had always craved, the money I had craved even more. . . . Instead of investigating Molly's death, I could do something else for her, something safe. I could carry her torch. I could be the ultimate sensitive male. I could be the new Molly Collins.

ABOUT THE AUTHOR

GARY PROVOST was the author of twenty-four books, including true crime, and more than a thousand newspaper and magazine articles. He appeared on *The Oprah Winfrey Show*, *Sally Jessy Raphael*, *A Current Affair*, and dozens of local television and radio shows.

BAFFLED IN BOSTON

A mystery

Gary Provost

BERKLEY PRIME CRIME, NEW YORK

BAFFLED IN BOSTON

A Berkley Prime Crime Book / published by arrangement with
the author

PRINTING HISTORY
Berkley Prime Crime edition / February 1996

The Putnam Berkley World Wide Web site address is
http://www.berkley.com

ISBN: 0-425-15183-2

Berkley Prime Crime Books are published
by The Berkley Publishing Group,
200 Madison Avenue, New York, NY 10016.
The name BERKLEY PRIME CRIME and the BERKLEY PRIME CRIME
design are trademarks belonging to Berkley Publishing Corporation.

PRINTED IN THE UNITED STATES OF AMERICA

10 9 8 7 6 5 4 3 2 1

Because I know how fortunate I am to have her as my wife, my honey, my lover, my pal, my playmate, my partner, my precious, precious darling, because my love for her is the overriding fact of my life, and because having her in my life is and will always be the best thing about it, I dedicate this book to Gail—a/k/a/ my darling little Nushka Resnikoff.

—G.P.
(a/k/a/ Major Garonovitch)

CHAPTER 1

On her way out the door my wife, Anne, said something about my choice of the freelance writing life being irresponsible, selfish, and unmanly. My unwillingness to wear a necktie was childish. My trips to Las Vegas were reckless. And most of her orgasms had been faked. Clearly, she was peeved. I was, she said, an utter failure. Also, she had fallen in love with another man, so she thought it would be best if she left me. It would turn out to be the second worst thing that happened that week.

For a year we had been living in a three-room apartment on the second floor of a brick building on Queensberry Street in Boston's Back Bay. It was a narrow little flat, the rooms all in a row like boxes, kind of like a three-room hall. Anne had complained about it often. She said that other people in their forties had houses. "Houses, Jeff," she used to say. "You know, with yards and garages."

That Sunday afternoon I followed Anne and her suitcases through the narrow bedroom, through the narrow living room, through the narrow kitchen, down

1

the narrow front stairs of the building, and out onto the brick steps which faced the narrow tree-lined street.

It was a Sunday in October, one of those chilly autumn afternoons, common in Massachusetts, with cold rain dripping like bad plumbing from a sky the color of nails. Pathetically defiant, I stood on the top step, getting wet while Anne shoved her luggage into her crumbling Volkswagen Jetta. "Utter failure, your ass!" I shouted, waving my arms in the air like Mussolini.

But it was a futile gesture. Anne fastened her seat belt, turned on her wipers, and pulled out of her parking space, banging someone's fender in the process. She did not look back.

Anne had also said, "Scotty, get yourself a real job," which had amused me because during the twelve years of our childless marriage, Anne, herself, had never stayed at one job long enough to need her pencil sharpened. Anne certainly had her faults. But still I loved her, and having the woman you love call you an utter failure just before she abandons you for another man is always stressful. As I watched her car shrink in the distance and finally disappear, it was like having a hole drilled in my heart.

I skipped the anger and denial steps and went directly to grief.

For the next few days I counted flowers on the wallpaper, watched television by the gallon, and smoked cigarettes, something I had not done in years. I even put my .38 Smith & Wesson to my head. Of course, I didn't load it. I wasn't that crazy.

During those first few days I mostly blamed Anne. I pretended that the main reason our marriage had ended was that I wanted children and she did not. If Anne were there, she would have argued that she couldn't very well quit work and have babies while I was earning less than a high school English teacher. However, Anne was not there, so I won all the arguments. But when I honestly inspected myself for answers, I could see that unfulfilled dreams had made shallow people of us both. I had become cynical, Anne skeptical. Perhaps Anne had left to get away from us.

By Wednesday I could sense a slight parting of the clouds, but I was still not ready for major life-affirming gestures. Like shaving, putting my socks in the laundry basket, or answering the phone. But I thought it would be a small vote for life if I could just change out of the ripe blue pajamas which I had been wearing for seventy-two hours, and into a fresh pair. So I took off the jammies and dropped them neatly onto the floor. And as I stood naked in the bedroom, searching for a clean pair of pajamas, Channel 4's Liz Walker came on TV with a bulletin.

"This just in to the Channel Four newsroom," she said. "Advice columnist Molly Collins has been struck by a hit-and-run driver in downtown Boston."

God, I thought. Not Molly. I felt my skin tighten around me.

"According to police, Collins, whose column is seen in fifteen hundred newspapers worldwide, was crossing Huntington Avenue in front of her apartment building when she was hit. Collins has been taken to Massachusetts General Hospital. We'll be back with more on this story at eleven, and we'll have today's winning Megabucks number."

I sat on my bed, stunned. Molly. My friend Molly had been smashed into by an automobile. What was God trying to pull here? First Anne, now Molly. I could not bear the thought of Molly in pain.

Still naked, I padded into my "office," a small corner of the living room about the size of a phone booth. I yanked away the blankets that I had placed over the phone to muffle its ring. I had not answered it since Anne's Sunday departure, and now a red light flashed impatiently on my answering machine, telling me that messages had come in. They would have to wait. I picked up the phone and dialed the hospital.

Good thing I'm not bleeding to death, I thought, when the hospital's phone rang for the fifteenth time. Molly. Was she bleeding to death? Jesus, how could this happen?

Finally I got through to someone officious who told me, "No visitors are allowed," and "No details are being released," and a lot of other things beginning with the word *No*. She talked to me as if I were just another reporter trying to get the story. She didn't understand. I was Molly's closest friend. At least, I had been at one time.

Time has a way of reshuffling the deck, I thought as I put the phone back on its cradle. I walked back into the bedroom. Mindlessly I got dressed, as if I were going somewhere. Somehow Molly and I had been reduced to eating lunch at a fern bar on Newbury Street every two months, and hardly even calling each other in the meantime. Now what pained me most about that was that, even though Molly was the busy, famous person, she was always asking me to visit, and it was I, the utter failure, who never seemed to make time for us.

As I stared at the television from which I had heard the news, my mind was filled with tragic pictures. Molly walking with a limp. Molly in a wheelchair. Molly in a grave.

"Damned drunk drivers!" I roared at the walls. "Hang them all."

How many news reports had I heard about some low-life from East Boston who had been arrested nine-teen times for drunk driving and not once put in jail? If they caught this brute and set him free, I would person-ally put a ball peen hammer to his head. Molly had never hurt anybody. It wasn't fair.

I was not only enraged at drunk drivers, I was mad at myself, too. It is the nature of us utter failures to cast our-selves into other people's dramas, and I couldn't get it out of my head that if I had accepted more dinner invitations from Molly, met her for more lunches, driven more often with her to Cape Cod, or taken her to more movies, my presence in her life would have shifted the time and place of all the other events in her life, and she would not have been in a certain spot at that moment when some drunken cretin sped by and smashed her down. It was a ridiculous thought, but no less painful for being so. I vowed that I would visit Molly every day that she was in the hospital.

By the time the eleven o'clock Eyewitness News came on, Molly had died.

"Like a sister to millions," Liz Walker was saying when the first pitiful wail came out of me.

"Messages of tribute have come in from Ann Landers and Abigail Van Buren," a correspondent on the scene at Mass. General was saying when I fell like a wounded animal to the floor of my bedroom and pounded my fists in rage.

"Funeral services to be held Saturday," Liz Walker said when my combined grief over the loss of Anne and Molly caused me, for the first time since I was a kid, to cry. It was the worse moment of my life.

I could not sleep. I smoked and smoked. I thought about the Smith & Wesson, but I didn't have the courage for that.

At three in the morning I stormed into my office like a crazy person, thinking that I would telephone everybody I knew. I was becoming unhinged and I needed the sound of friendly voices to lead me back to reality.

Instead, I settled for the answering machine. Yes, I thought, I'll play my messages. Reminders of friends, of my work, will prove that life goes on. Maybe Anne had called and wanted to come back.

There were no Sunday calls. The first call was from Monday, a Mrs. Spicer at First Boston Bank. Discreetly she had left no message except her phone number. But I knew what she wanted; it was the same thing she always wanted. I had overdrawn my checking account. Checks were bouncing all over the state, and the bank was curious about how I planned to handle it.

Then there were a couple of hang-ups, and a Tuesday night call from some guy in Methuen who wanted me to critique his manuscript about bone fishing. Then two more hang-ups. Then I heard Molly's voice and I started to cry again.

"Scotty, it's Molly. Look, sweetie, I'm giving a big party a week from Saturday and it's really important to me that you come. Bring Anne if you want. No excuses, okay? It's sort of a surprise party. Call me in the morning. If I'm not at the office, call me at home. I'll be soaking in a hot bathtub. Some numbskull nearly ran me over tonight, and I think I wrenched my back jumping out of the way. Talk to you soon. Love you."

Somebody had almost run Molly over on Tuesday night. And tonight she had been killed by a hit-and-run driver. Maybe in my grief I was just getting paranoid, but as I cried for Molly and for myself, I couldn't get it out of my mind that she had been hit deliberately.

Murdered.

CHAPTER 2

I met Molly a few years before my career went sour. I met her at the *Bay State News,* an aggressive suburban daily that was giving the Boston papers fits. Molly was the paper's advice columnist, and I, then with a growing reputation as a writer of true crime books, was a guest speaker for the newspaper's editorial staff. When Molly and I met, the attraction was immediate. We both loved the Boston Celtics, fried chicken, and Bugs Bunny. Neither of us could stomach John McEnroe or the Moral Majority. Like a couple of tots, we became friends instantly. We were both married at the time, and we never mistook our friendship for a romance.

A year after Molly and I met, she divorced her sexist swine of a husband. At that time Anne and I were looking for an apartment. My friend, Mungus, who also had gotten divorced, was looking for new quarters, too, and so was Molly's friend, Deidre. So we all decided to live together.

We rented a respectable looking six-room split-level house in a Brady Bunch neighborhood in Framingham. Group living, we called it. It was common in those inflationary years. Friends would live together and share the electric bill, the phone, the heat, the rent, so that everybody could live in a roomy house instead of several small apartments. More important, none of us had kids, and this was our way of having family.

Molly and I used to go for walks every day on that quiet block, where station wagons sat in almost every driveway. Molly would wear those billowing olive-colored slacks of hers and her wiry black hair would blow out in all directions. The neighbors always smiled at us, thinking we were a couple. And I guess we were. It was always Molly to whom I went with my problems. With Molly I could reveal fears and weaknesses that I had always kept from Anne. Anne and Molly, always cordial, but never close, seemed to sense that they were in each other's way, but nobody ever spoke about it. Molly and I talked about our careers. We always thought that I would be the one to become famous. Who would have guessed that Molly Collins would become a household name.

From the *Bay State News*, Molly went to the *Boston Patriot,* replacing the advice columnist Lillian Gilmartin. When the *Patriot* began to syndicate a few of their columnists nationally, Molly soared. By the time Molly died, her column was being published in twenty countries. She was as big as Ann Landers and Dear Abby, mainly because she was different from them. When they were square, she was hip. When they were conservative, she was radical. When they said to keep cool, she said to take risks. People loved her. And she looked great on television.

I thought of all this a million times during the month after Molly's death. I spent that month somewhat grief-stricken, somewhat drunk. Then one morning over a bowl of Cracklin' Oats I understood that self-pity was not fun, and I decided to no longer live alone in the apartment I had shared with Anne.

I called Mungus and asked if it would be okay if I lived with him for a while.

"Does the Pope shit in the woods?" Mungus replied.

I took that as a yes, and on a November evening I gutted my apartment and drove up to Plum Island, just over the causeway from Newburyport. A one-hour drive north of Boston, Plum is a flat and narrow island, eleven miles long, much of it sandy beach. A sanctuary for migrating birds and malicious greenflies, it is a place where Bostonians who hate Cape Cod, and New Hampshirites who hate Hampton Beach, can hide out for a week in the summer. I had gone there often to visit Mungus. Anne had come along once, but the greenflies had made her testy, and she had vowed never to come again. Because I wanted Mungus and Plum Island to myself, I never told Anne that the greenflies only harass people for two weeks in July.

Mungus's cottage went by the name of "Late Sleeper." The words were painted in faded red letters on a piece of driftwood that was nailed over the front door. "Late Sleeper" was two stories of weathered slatboards that tilted a dozen different ways. It looked like the rough sketch for one of Mungus's cartoons. The cottage just barely stood on the corner of Ocean Drive and an unpaved road that exhaled clouds of sandy brown dust whenever anybody drove on it. But, in the win column, you could walk out the front door, cross the street, and be on the beach in twenty-five seconds.

It was already dark when I pulled into the dirt lot beside the cottage, being careful not to run over Mungus's flowers. He came out in a sweatsuit and helped me carry my stuff up creaky stairs to the cramped, slanty-walled bedroom that would be my home.

When we finished unloading, I stood in the room, surrounded by a dozen ratty cardboard cartons that contained everything I owned except my car, and somewhat baffled by all the sudden changes in my life. From the cluttered room I could smell both the ocean and the bay that was just a few blocks behind the cottage. If I want to drown myself, I thought, I won't have far to walk.

Mungus held a can of Coors beer tightly in his right hand and said, "This is great. We'll hang around and do manly stuff. It will be fantastic. It will be like being back in college."

I didn't remind Mungus that I had never attended college, and that he had been thrown out of Colgate for moral lapses. That was not his point. As I plucked my possessions from cardboard boxes and found places for them in the small room, I felt as if I were maneuvering around a friendly bear. Mungus is a good-sized fellow. His real name is Hugh, so his sisters used to call him Humongous, which evolved into Mungus. "Think of the money we'll save on video rentals," Mungus said. He took a swig of his beer.

"Right," I said, hardly listening. My mind was elsewhere. I had gone through the horror of Molly's funeral without falling completely apart, and I had told no one about my suspicion that Molly had been murdered, believing I would be thought insane. But now I was aching to tell Mungus, so that he could tell me it was an idiotic idea.

"And pizza deliveries," Mungus said.

"Pizza deliveries?" I said. I placed some socks in a drawer.

"We can split the tip," he explained.

"Great," I said somberly.

Certainly Mungus could use the rent money I would give him. He did not have a real job. The cottage, on one side, had a small studio with its own entrance, and Mungus, in violation of the island's zoning ordinances, used the studio as his business, T-Shirt Heaven. There he sold T-shirts and sweatshirts, on which he would print anything the customer wanted, no matter how disgusting or libelous it might be, though Mungus did draw the line at racist slogans. Mungus, who offered a twenty-percent discount for anti-Republican sentiments, specialized in small letters. He once printed an entire haftorah on the T-shirt of a bar mitzvah boy and then gave the shirt to the kid for free, though Mungus did show up at the bar mitzvah, where he ate more than eighty dollars' worth of food. Free food was a big thing with Mungus. Anyhow, T-Shirt Heaven had long been about as solvent as your average Texas savings and loan institution, and Mungus's career as a cartoonist rarely raked in enough money even to pay for his season tickets to the Bruins.

Mungus watched with great curiosity while I silently shoved my clothes into the dark wooden dresser. Neurotically searching for order in my life, I placed socks and underwear in two small drawers on top, shirts in the middle drawer, pants in the bottom. It occurred to me, as I began closing drawers, that I couldn't remember Anne ever folding my clothes or hanging them up, the way other guys' wives did. But then, I had never checked her transmission fluid, either.

For many seconds I stared down at the remaining boxes as if I had never seen them. Would Anne have murdered Molly for any reason? It was not a new or surprising thought. During the month since Molly's death

I had interrogated, in my mind, a list of possible suspects ranging from the doorman at Molly's building to Dr. Ruth.

"Scotty," Mungus said, "you are not with the game plan tonight. What's on your mind?"

"Nothing," I said.

"I believe that," Mungus said.

"Okay, there's something I've got to tell you."

Mungus raised one of his big bushy eyebrows.

"Sounds serious," he said.

"It's about Molly."

"Shit," he said.

Mungus had not been as close to Molly as I, but he had lived with her in that Framingham house.

"I don't want to talk about Molly," he said. "It gives me the creeps thinking about her being dead. How can a person be dead? I don't get it." Now he put his beer can on my dresser. He leaned against the wall and pulled one of his beefy hands against the other. "Isometrics," he explained.

"The night she died she left a message on my answering machine," I told him. "She said that she had almost been hit by a car."

Mungus thought it over. "So?"

"Don't you find that strange? She was almost hit by a car one night and the next night she *was* hit by a car?"

"Not especially," Mungus said. He pulled his hands apart and shadow-boxed for a minute. Then he sat on the bed, which screeched under his weight. He hauled one of my cartons onto his lap, ripped it open, and started pulling out its contents. "Gore Vidal?" he shrieked, holding a paperback with two fingers, as if it were evidence. "You're reading books by Gore Vidal?"

"My wife's," I lied. "And you're changing the subject.

Now listen. Molly gets almost killed by a car one night, and the next night she actually does get killed, and you're saying you don't find that to be an astounding coincidence?"

"Not at all," Mungus said. He continued plucking items out of the cartons as if they were his own.

"Why not?"

Mungus peered into one of my paperbacks, read a few sentences, then put the book down.

"For starters," he said, "it's not like Molly was in downtown Marblehead or something. She was in Boston, where crazed drivers foaming at the mouth are easier to find than parking spaces. I was there Saturday and I must have had five near-death experiences just trying to get across Kenmore Square. Not only that, but you know how Molly was, always thinking of something else, not watching where she was going."

By this time Mungus was surrounded by my audio-tapes, my tennis balls, and photographs of the minor celebrities I had interviewed.

"Maybe you're right," I said. "But it bothers me."

"Of course it bothers you," Mungus said. "She was our main gal. Remember, we used to call her that."

"Yes."

Mungus put the carton aside. He seemed bored with looking at my stuff. "Besides, what's your point? I mean what are you saying? That she could have been hit on purpose?"

"Well, yes. Silly me. I'm just being paranoid, right?"

"Right," Mungus said. "Who would want to kill Molly? It's absurd. Kill an advice columnist. That would be like killing Pat Sajak. What would be the point?"

"You're probably right," I said. I almost believed it.

"But let's pretend that somebody would want to kill Molly. Who would it be?"

"Nobody," Mungus said. "There is nobody who would murder Molly Collins."

"Nobody?"

"Oh, some strung-out teenage crackhead sleaze sociopath who needed a new pair of Nikes might kill her to steal her pocketbook or something, but that's tough to do when you're driving a car. Nobody would kill Molly, not the way you mean."

"Why?"

"Because Molly was great," Mungus said. "The killer would have to be a psycho."

"Well, just pretend there is such a psycho."

"There isn't," Mungus said.

"Mungus," I said, "humor me. Pretend there's a murderer. Who would it be?"

Mungus stared off into space. His eyebrows did a couple of loops and spins. "Lillian Gilmartin," he finally said.

"Lillian Gilmartin?" I said, sounding astounded, even though the thought had occurred to me often.

Lillian Gilmartin had been the advice columnist at the *Boston Patriot* until she was replaced by Molly. Now she was the advice columnist for the competing *Boston Times*. Well-known locally, she had never achieved national syndication. It was no secret that the writer of "Luv, Lilly" thought that Molly's fame and fortune should have been her own. But their feud had always been, it seemed to me, mainly a creation of each paper's public relations department.

"Lillian Gilmartin?" I said again.

"Sure," Mungus said. "Isn't it obvious?"

"You're saying that Lillian Gilmartin might have killed Molly."

"No," Mungus said. "I'm saying no one deliberately killed her. I'm saying that if I believed that Molly was murdered, which I don't, I'd give a lot of thought to Miss Lillian."

"Why?" I asked.

"Because she hated Molly. Everybody knows that."

"Maybe," I said. "But even if she did, why now, after six years?"

"I don't know," Mungus said. "Maybe she just got a bad case of PMS one night and did it. And by the way, why did you place rolled-up socks in your drawer instead of shooting them in from across the room like Larry Bird? What's bugging you tonight?"

"You mean besides the fact that my friend is dead, my wife left me, and my career has been dog shit for four years?"

"Yeah, besides all that?"

"What's bugging me is that I wanted you to talk me out of this idea that Molly was murdered."

"She wasn't murdered, okay?"

"Thanks," I said, "but I can't shake it."

"So what are you going to do?" Mungus said. He glanced at the doorway. I knew he was wondering whether or not this was an appropriate time to go downstairs for another beer.

"I don't know. I was thinking of calling Joan Bentley."

"Molly's secretary?"

"Yes, just ask her a few questions. See if she remembers anything odd."

"Aha!" Mungus said.

"What?"

"So that's what this is all about. This whole thing is

just an excuse to call Joan Bentley because you kind of fancy her."

"Don't be ridiculous."

"You've always fancied her, don't deny it," Mungus said. He rose triumphantly from the bed and moved toward the door. His hand already assumed the shape of the next beer can he would hold.

"She's married, for God's sake."

"Oh, excuse me," Mungus said. "I had forgotten you were a man of such high moral standards."

"Joan has nothing to do with this," I said. "I'm really afraid that Molly was murdered. Is that so hard to understand?"

"It sounds . . ."

"I know, I know," I said, "it sounds crazy."

"Right," Mungus said. "*Crazy* is the word we were looking for. You win the trip to Luxembourg and the set of Samsonite luggage." He poked me in the stomach. "You want a drink while you finish unpacking?"

"Sure," I said.

Instead of leaving, he stood beside me for a moment without speaking. In his eyes I saw a look that was almost fatherly. It was as if he could see me walking into danger and wanted to pull me back, but didn't know how. For the moment he seemed larger than usual, mainly because I, with my sadness and my failures, felt small enough to hide in a hamper.

"Jesus, she's really dead, isn't she," he finally said. Then he turned and moved heavily toward the door.

A few minutes later he came back up the stairs with a new Coors for him and a wine cooler for me. He sat on the bed again and we talked about other things while I pulled the remnants of my life from the cartons piece by piece and hung them in the closet, dropped them on the dresser, or placed them near the staircase so that I could later take them down to the small front room that would be my office.

When it was time for David Letterman, Mungus got ready to leave my room. He put his arm around me and leaned in close. It reminded me of kinder days when he and I used to play flag football on the green in Framingham. Back then Mungus would pull me close the same way, so that other guys couldn't hear the secret plays he would whisper, plays which always ended with the promise, "That'll shove lye up their asses."

Now, in the small bedroom, with its slanted walls that seemed to slice into me like blades, Mungus said, "Look, I've got to be honest with you. I don't like talking about Molly. It makes me cold. But yeah, I find it strange that she was almost hit by a car the night before she died. Real strange. I can't imagine that anybody would want to murder her, but this planet is a very strange place and you never know."

"What do you think I should do?" I said.

"I don't know." He shrugged. "All I know is that you've had your throat slashed once and that seems like enough for one lifetime. There's a lot of freaks out there. Watch yourself."

Mungus's allusion to throat-slashing was prescient. It had been on my mind. Four years earlier I had published *Soul of Darkness,* my third true crime book. My first two had been well reviewed and quite successful. But this one, the reviewers agreed, could best be used to line cat boxes. It was the story of Fred McHale, the mass murderer. McHale was a Unitarian minister who answered a chilling "yes" to every question at his trial, including "Did you mutilate and behead six women in Muncie, Indiana?" He did not relish his fame. When the book was published, McHale broke out of prison and dropped by for a visit one night when Anne, fortunately, was away. There he terrorized me for six hours with the gleaming blade of an eight-inch carving knife, before sliding the knife across my throat and then shoving it into his own black heart. I lived, he died.

Though I later told the story heroically in many fine Boston saloons, the truth is that I was terrified for every single minute of that six-hour ordeal, and when it ended, I was left shaken and cowardly and unwilling ever again to research a story involving violent or deranged people. My encounter with him had also left me with an obsessive fear of sharp blades, and lately even butter knives were making me edgy.

Mungus and I watched television in the living room. Then I went to bed for the first time in my new nest. Mungus was a good guy, I thought, and I would try to be a good housemate to him.

I thought the sound of the ocean would lull me into the peaceful sleep which I had craved ever since Anne left. But I did not sleep that night. The new home. The things on my mind. Something about my conversation with Mungus was troubling me. As Molly would have said, some need of mine had not been met. I tossed. I turned. In the darkness the walls were no longer slanted. Everything was flat and black. I thought, of course, about Molly and how everybody loved her.

Actually, not everybody loved Molly, I thought as I endured that first sleepless night in Mungus's cottage. But I loved her. To millions of people Molly Collins had been "Dear Molly," the voice of wisdom. But to me she was the shy person who was a nervous wreck before she had to give a speech, the divorced woman who was terrified that she would never find true love, the perceptive but often insecure friend who used to call me and say, "Scotland, I need help. Give me some advice."

By four in the morning my face was wet from tears, and I understood why my conversation with Mungus had been so unsatisfying. I didn't want him to convince me that Molly had not been murdered. I wanted him to tell me that it was okay for me to be a coward.

I was getting sucked into the fantasy that I could figure out who killed my Molly and why. But I was scared. My throat had already been slashed once, and that's why I hadn't written a true crime book in four years, that's why my career was a wreck. All this time I had steered clear of psychos and sharp blades. I certainly didn't need another Fred McHale in my life now.

Molly wouldn't make me do this, I told myself as I twisted this way and that on my new bed. Molly would say, "Take care of yourself, Scotland, let the police handle this." And she'd be right. It wasn't my job to bring her killer to justice.

But the police didn't think there was anything to be handled, except a hit-and-run. I knew there was nobody to take care of Molly. And if Molly's friend, the washed-up investigative reporter, couldn't look into her murder, then who could?

CHAPTER 3

On the morning after my talk with Mungus I drove to Boston to meet the young cop who had investigated Molly's hit-and-run case. He was an eager pup, Norman something, and he told me what I already knew. The chances of the driver being caught were about the same as the chances of the Red Sox signing an all-star pitcher whose arm didn't turn to swill the following season.

"Hit-and-run drivers don't leave calling cards," Norman said cleverly. When I told him about the message on my answering machine, he pulled out the accident report to see if there was something that he had overlooked. Nothing.

"As you know," he said, "we can't start a homicide investigation on something like that." He said "as you know," twelve times, and it was obvious that he knew who I was, or, more accurately, who I had been, and still thought of me as a writer of true crime books. When we were done, he asked for my autograph. My next step in the investigation was to call Joan Bentley and ask her to meet me for breakfast.

Which is why I was sitting in the Creamery coffee

shop on Boylston Street in Boston at eight-fifteen on Monday morning, a morning that was so dreary it should have been condemned.

The restaurant was filled with earnest young working people. They sat at small glass tables under dangling fake plants. They clinked saucers and cups and pressed their noses into folded-up copies of *The Wall Street Journal.*

"Scotty," I heard Joan Bentley call.

Looking up from my *USA Today,* I saw Joan. Her face glowed. She stood just inside the door to the restaurant. From there she waved to me as she daintily shook raindrops from her blue umbrella. I felt myself smile, something I hadn't done much lately.

Joan wove her way toward me between rows of tables. She was small, slim, mysteriously feminine, and she moved fluidly, as if she were a teenager on Rollerblades. I stood to greet her. Joan greeted me with a kiss, then laughed nervously.

"I'd better be careful about where I'm seen kissing strange men," she said. "My husband's patients are everywhere." Joan's husband was either a chiropractor or a proctologist; I couldn't remember which, but I knew it had prac or proc in it.

I sat down. Joan slipped off her coat and draped it over the back of her chair. She wore a tight tangerine-colored sweater that fit snugly around her breasts, and a long peasant skirt that went down to her ankles and was far more stirring than any miniskirt. What would she think of my shocking revelation? I wondered. Would she believe that her boss had been murdered?

"Sorry I'm late," she said. "Had to help my son with some last-minute homework."

This was the reality check I needed, I thought. A reminder that Joan had not only a husband, but a kid.

Instead of sitting across from me, Joan sat to my right, crossed her legs, folded her hands on the table, and leaned toward me. I shifted my chair slightly so that I could be inches closer to her, but then I felt like an embarrassed schoolboy and I pulled back a bit. I was afraid that if she touched me I would get all weepy. She stared straight at me, her eyes shining.

"I was in the library the other day," she said. "I looked you up in *Books in Print*."

"Why?" I asked.

"I don't know," she said. "It was fun to see the name of somebody I actually know."

I smiled. "Joan, your boss was one of the most famous women in America."

"I know," Joan said. "But . . ." She blushed. "It was like being with you. Anyhow, they had all your books listed. Why did you stop writing true crimes? I love true crimes."

"One of my subjects tried to remove my esophagus with a steak knife," I said.

"Really?"

"It made me a bit shy about dealing with criminals."

I had told the Fred McHale story many times, but never, apparently, to Joan. Over the years I had repeated the story so often that it had begun to sound like the Pledge of Allegiance. So now I gave Joan the short version, leaving out the part about pissing in my pants. I also didn't tell Joan that the McHale incident was the point at which, at least in my mind, everything started to go to hell. It was after the critics had slashed my book and McHale had slashed my throat that my career went backward. Instead of writing another book, I had returned to writing for magazines, which doesn't pay diddly, and writing short stories, which doesn't pay at all. My income had dropped. My marriage had decayed.

After I told my McHale story, Joan gazed at me as if I had just plunged a lance into a dragon.

"You must have been frightened," she said.

"Frightened? I laugh at danger," I said.

We fiddled with our menus for a moment. I held mine close and squinted. I certainly wasn't going to let an attractive woman know that I owned reading glasses. Then the waitress came and took Joan's tea order and refilled my coffee cup.

Should I tell her now? I wondered. *Molly was murdered, Joan.* Get it out of the way, and then enjoy breakfast? Or should I wait, just slip it into the conversation later? *Oh, by the way, Joan, Molly's death was no accident, it was murder.*

"What do you want to do today?" Joan asked.

When I had called Joan and asked her to meet me for breakfast, I hadn't planned on anything except asking her questions about Molly. Now, finding myself nervous in her presence, I knew I wanted more. When Mungus had so quaintly suggested that I "fancied" Joan, he was, in his own clumsy way, accurate. I would have phrased it differently, but the reality was: my wife had left me, Joan was pretty, my hormones were bubbling like beef stew all the way up to my earlobes, and being with Joan had always made me happy, which is why I had avoided being with her for so long. I pushed it from my mind, or tried to. I wasn't here to tell Joan how much I liked her. I was here to ask about Molly.

"Don't you have to go to work today?" I asked.

"Well, no," Joan said. "I took the day off. I thought we might go someplace, the way we used to."

Joan, apparently had not forgotten me. Three years

earlier I had met her at an author lecture in Harvard Square. Afterward, she had invited me to one of those Cambridge coffee shops, where we laughed because we could get thirty-seven kinds of espresso, but couldn't get just a regular cup of coffee. The next day we had a picnic at the Arnold Arboretum, where we kept ourselves warm with a thermos of hot coffee and a few adolescent kisses. It never went beyond that, though we both wanted it to. But we stayed in touch. It was I who introduced Joan to Molly, and when Molly's secretary ran away with the circulation manager, the job went to Joan, who had once been secretary of the year for Middlesex County.

"Sure, we can go someplace," I said now. "Let's order some breakfast and then decide."

Now what do I do, I thought, take her to the Museum of Science? Joan was toying with her wedding ring, and I could sense that this was not the best time to tell her I had called to ask questions about another woman. I gazed around at the clusters of sweet-smelling wage earners. How did they handle inner conflict? I wondered. The waitress returned and we ordered breakfast. While we waited for our food, Joan pulled a compact mirror out of her pocketbook and fussed with her hair. Would she think I was crazy? I wondered. Except for Mungus and Norman the cop, I had shared with no one my belief that Molly had been murdered.

When breakfast came I picked at it. Lately I'd been getting heartburn from every meal. In fact, since the loss of the two women in my life, my health seemed to be in constant peril. Every night I would wake up, my chest filled with fire, and my muddled mind convinced that I had something that was one hundred percent fatal.

While we ate, Joan and I made small talk. We talked first about Joan's job at the *Boston Patriot*.

"They've got me checking ads in classified," she said. "They say they're going to give me my old job back as soon as they replace Molly. God knows how they plan to do that."

Then we talked about Joan's husband, the practor. He had become distant and neglectful, steeped in his work and hardly aware that he had a family. Joan said she wished that things were the way they used to be. I told Joan about my wife's departure. Joan said she was sorry to hear it, but I found myself hoping that she wasn't.

"Sometimes I think I should just have an affair and forget about trying to improve my marriage," she said.

She looked into my eyes.

"That would probably be the best solution," I told her. "At least until your kid is grown." I gazed mindlessly at the plastic plants that hung from steel hooks on the Creamery's ceiling. What, I wondered, would Dear Abby think of such advice?

And we talked about Joan's son, Peter. Peter, I gathered, was obnoxious, though Joan did not use that word. He was thinking of quitting high school because he knew he was smarter than other kids and also because he wanted to piss off his father.

"Peter's never gotten much attention from his father," Joan said, "and now he's got it in his mind that by quitting school he can punish his father. What do you think I should do?"

"Well," I said, sitting up straighter, the way you do when someone asks for your advice, "you could point out to Peter that if his father told him to quit school and he did, then he would be letting his father control his behavior. If his father tells him not to quit school and Peter quits because of that, then he's still letting his father control his behavior. Make Peter realize that if he quits, his father wins. That will keep him in school."

All the worry drained from Joan's face, and she reached over the table and caressed my hand.

"Thank you," she said. "I'll talk to him."

Joan continued to talk. She seemed hungry for attention. I liked listening to her. Joan was originally from Nebraska or Kansas, one of those states where the boys drive tractors by the time they are seven, and her accent always made me think of summer nights on the front porch of a farmhouse, even though I had never actually spent a summer night on the front porch of a farmhouse. Now, with my terrible belief about Molly's death haunting me, I felt comforted as Joan told me about the ordinary things in her life, movies she had seen alone, and books she had read. I think she was lonely. At one point she leaned forward and took my hand. "Gee," she said, "it's really good to see you."

I wondered if she had any idea of how lonely I was.

After we ate, the waitress pulled our plates away and left the check on my side of the table. I was on my third coffee. Joan was sipping tea.

"Tell me about Molly," I finally said. "I mean just before she died. I didn't see much of her during the last six months."

"I know," Joan said. "She talked a lot about you. Molly thought the world of you."

It was a kind comment, but I felt as if Joan had reached over and stabbed me with a fork.

"She was happy," Joan said. "She was getting ready for a big party. I was sending out the invitations."

I remembered about the party. The last time I had heard Molly's voice it had been on my answering machine, inviting me to the party.

"Why the big party?" I asked. "Molly was not exactly the Mad Hatter."

"I'm sure she had a reason," Joan said. "There were more than a hundred invitations."

"I think she was murdered," I said suddenly. Great investigator, Scotty, I thought. Real subtle.

"Murdered?" Joan said. Her hand trembled around her teacup. She paled, then placed the cup on the table and pushed it away from her.

"Yes."

"Murdered?" she said again. "How could that be?"

I told Joan about the message on my answering machine, the first car incident. She looked stunned.

"Hit deliberately?" she said, almost in a whisper. "It never crossed my mind."

"Because it doesn't make any sense," I said. "I mean can you think of any reason why someone would want to kill an advice columnist?"

"No. Well, yes, I guess. Jealousy."

"Jealousy?"

"Yes," she said. She was still shaking.

"You mean Lillian Gilmartin."

"Lillian? Oh, no, that's not what I mean. I mean that everybody thinks he's great at giving advice. But Molly was getting hundreds of thousands of dollars for doing it. Every day we got letters from people saying they could do a better job than Molly."

"Killing her wouldn't help," I said.

"It would help the person who gets her job," Joan said. Her voice sounded hollow, as if she had taken this new possibility and gone back in her mind to review everything she knew about Molly's death.

"Who's that?" I said.

"Huh?"

"Who gets Molly's job?"

"I don't know," Joan said. "Somebody at the paper, I'm sure."

Yes, I thought, somebody nuts. Somebody who would be thrilled to finish Fred McHale's handiwork on my throat if I asked too many questions.

I let a moment pass while Joan absorbed the fact that we were really talking about murder. And then I asked, "Is there anything at all? Anything odd about the way Molly acted, or anything strange at the newspaper before she died?"

"No. Nothing that I can think of," Joan said sadly. "Except that, well, Arnold Lansky is never there anymore," she said.

Lansky was the publisher of the *Boston Patriot*. He was an old-style newspaperman who refused to run lottery stories and had turned down liquor advertising for years.

"Why not?" I asked.

"Everybody says the paper is going broke and he's going to have to sell it," Joan said.

"Who'd buy it?" I asked.

"Lawrence Dracut, maybe."

Dracut, well known in New England, already owned four newspapers and three radio stations. He was not known for high journalistic standards. His style was to buy a paper, run it himself for several months so that everybody could get used to putting color pictures of corpses on the front page, and then go on to the next acquisition.

"Some people think Dracut and Mr. Lansky have already come to an agreement and Dracut is running the *Patriot* by telephone," Joan said. "Mr. Lansky is just staying until Dracut comes on the job."

It made sense. The *Patriot* had lately been showing subtle, but steady, signs of pandering. One local rape victim, who would have been "a mother of two," "a saleswoman," or "a Cambridge resident" in the *Boston Times,* was daily described in the *Patriot* as "a former beauty queen."

"Anything else interesting going on?"

"No," Joan said. "That's it." And then, "So it's important to you to find out if somebody did murder Molly?"

"It's something I have to do," I said.

"For Molly?"

"Yes."

"I don't think that's what Molly would want you to do," she said.

"No?"

"I think Molly would want you to go back to writing true crime books. Because that's what you're good at," Joan said. And then, as if it somehow followed, she said, "You must be lonely with your wife gone."

"Very," I said.

"Me, too," she said very softly, to herself.

By nine-thirty there were only a few people left in the Creamery. Everybody else had gone to work. The waitress came by, but I waved her off. I knew that if I drank another cup of coffee, I would have heartburn for the rest of the day and I would think it was cardiac arrest. Through the window of the coffee shop I could see that the sky was still gray, the color of my life. My questions about Molly had gotten us nowhere, but Joan and I had spent the time sharing memories of Molly. Small things now seemed precious to us. We both missed her terribly. Now Joan had gone quiet. She stared pensively out at the morning. I was touched by how lovely and vulnerable she looked.

"Thanks for the advice," she said.

"Huh?"

"About my son."

"Oh."

Another moment passed.

"Scotty, did you want to see me so you could ask questions about Molly?"

"Not just that," I said. I could feel my hand trembling.

"Oh?"

"My friend Mungus says I fancy you."

"Really?"

"Really," I said. She smiled again.

Joan reached over and took my hand again. It felt good to be touched, and I appreciated it and I wanted to say something to her about Molly, something poignant about the loss we had both suffered. I wanted to somehow connect the two of us with our shared sadness. But when I opened my mouth, the words that came out were, "I know what I'd like to do today."

"What?"

"I'd like to hold you," I said.

I knew there was no chance that Joan and I would go somewhere and hold each other and not make love, also, but I had said what I really wanted.

Molly would not approve of this, I thought. Not because Joan was a married woman. Molly could accept that. She would disapprove because she would know what I knew, that my chances of making Joan Bentley's life less lonely were not as good as my chances of becoming governor of Wyoming. But Molly, I thought, I need some affection and you're not here to give it to me.

"That would be very nice," Joan said.

I dished out some money for the check, and Joan put her coat on. We left the restaurant and drove to a state park in Natick. There we held each other in the car, listening to the radio and the rain, and hardly talking. But we both needed more, and when the holding turned to kissing, we looked into each other's eyes and came to an understanding. So I pulled out of the park and drove west on the Massachusetts Turnpike, thinking that before we checked into a motel it would be best to put some miles between us and Boston, where Joan's husband did his doctoring. Along the way I noticed that a car in front of us had an NRA sticker on the rear window, and it occurred to me—probably because I'd been talking about Fred McHale—that Joan's husband could be one of those gun enthusiasts you hear about on *A Current Affair* who massacres his wife and her lover in the motel room to which he has followed them.

At the Framingham-Marlboro exit I pulled off the turnpike and drove over to Route 9. Across from The Steak House I drove into the parking lot of a motel called Carefree Villa, a very Italian sort of establishment with pink flamingos painted on the outside walls. Joan and I acted like criminals. I went in alone and registered with the clerk, who, mercifully, did not run my MasterCard through one of those machines that would have told him I was over my limit. When I got back to the car, Joan was touching up her makeup. "Room seven," I whispered, as if the parking lot might be bugged. Then I went to the room and waited for her. I was a nervous wreck. It felt as if several ice ages had passed since the last time I'd made love with a woman other than my wife.

When Joan got to the room, there were awkward moments while I stalled. I fiddled idiotically with the television dial, as if we had come to watch *Wheel of*

Fortune or something. Then I checked to see if the air conditioner was working, though only an Eskimo would use it on such a chilly day. Finally Joan went into the bathroom, then came out a few minutes later wearing nothing but a towel, a smile, and perfume.

Shyly she slipped under the covers of the king-size bed, then, in an awkward attempt at flirtation, she tossed the towel out to me.

"Come on in," she said nervously, "the water's fine."

I realized then that I had forgotten about Molly. The anticipation of lovemaking with Joan had nudged Molly from my mind for the first time since her death. I felt disloyal. Molly. God, what would she say about this?

Dear Molly, I thought, *I'm in a motel room with a woman who is quite sexy and lovely and as lonely as I am, and she's ready to make love with me because she really likes me and has no idea that I am a washed-up loser. But she's married and has a kid, and I'm not exactly a man with a bright future. What should I do? Signed, Lonely and Horny.*

I knew Molly would respond with something insanely principled like, Dear L. and H., you must tell this woman the truth first, that you see no happy ending for this affair, then see if she still wants to go to bed with you.

Great. The truth. I couldn't tell Joan a thing like that. Not now. Anybody who's ever had an erection can tell you that once the door is locked and the woman's eyes are sparkling with desire, it is far too late for honesty. I'd had my chance to reject Joan at the Creamery. Now was not a good time to reconsider. We were talking here about a sweet, beautiful woman who adored me and was anxious to have me in her arms. It would be ridiculous to now throw it all away for a principle. I did, however, remove from my wallet two condoms which had been there since the Bicentennial, and I placed them on the table beside the bed. I might be weak, I thought, but I'm not stupid. Joan's blue eyes beckoned. I undressed and crawled in next to her.

For three hours we made love, first the slippery, grinding, screaming kind, then later the tender, cooing, sleepy kisses kind. I like both kinds. Not surprisingly, I was a lot more durable than I had been in years with Anne. Joan was a new woman with new smells to be inhaled, new curves to be explored. Also, it had been a long time since the sap had been tapped, and my appetite for affection was as deep and keenly felt as Joan's.

When I was no longer inside Joan, she clung to me like a frightened child. It was touching to see her so vulnerable, and it was scary. When I caressed her, her body quivered like a petal, as if she had not been cuddled for years. She lay with her head on me, her long hair splashing across my chest. I could feel my heart beating against her cheek. We both needed to be held. It was not lost on me that we had both been reminded recently of our vulnerability in the world, of our mortality, and that despite any lies that I told Joan or lies she told herself, there was a transcendent honesty in what we were doing. Or maybe that was self-serving bullshit. I wasn't really sure.

Before Joan fell asleep in my arms, with her head now pushed deep onto my chest, and the sweet smell of her hair rising to me with every breath, she said, "Do you think we're going to fall in love?"

"You never know," I said. "You never know."

Later, though I lay with a beautiful woman snuggled asleep in my arms, my mood darkened. Why did I have to say a thing like that? I wondered. I thought about Anne, Molly, Joan.

After an hour like this, with Joan's head riding peacefully on the rising and falling of my chest, she stirred and stroked me softly.

"I think it's wonderful that you want to do something for Molly," she said sleepily. "But maybe it really was just a hit-and-run driver. Maybe you're overreacting. Maybe this investigation is your way of keeping Molly alive."

When I got back to Plum Island, Mungus was not home. There was a message on my machine from Joe "Crash" Galovitch at the *Patriot*.

Crash was director of public relations for the *Patriot*, but I knew him from the days when I was freelancing in Miami, and he had his own small public relations agency down there. Over the years we had stayed in occasional touch, and lately I'd run into him a few times at the Foxwoods casino in Connecticut.

When I got Crash on the phone, we went through the "How the hell are you?" formalities, and then Crash said, "Scotty, I need a major, major favor." As always, everything that Crash said sounded like an announcement.

"Name it."

"It's this Molly Collins thing. I need you to stop snooping around like Sherlock Holmes."

"Who told you?" I asked. It seemed to me that there were only three possible people: Mungus, Norman, or Joan.

"Joan Bentley told me," Crash said.

"Joan?" I said. I was hurt. "I just dropped her at her car an hour ago. What did she do, take a jet home?"

"That's not important," Crash said. "But there's two things that are important. One is that you are totally wrong on this thing. Molly was not murdered. She was hit by some Neanderthal in a car. It's tragic as hell, but not murder. I know you were close to her and all, but you're way off on this murder thing. It's all those true crime books you wrote. You think everything is murder."

"How do you know it wasn't?"

"Well, I don't know for sure," Crash said. "Anything's possible, I suppose. But if Molly were murdered, there would have to be something bizarre going on in her personal life, because it sure as hell didn't have anything to do with her work here."

"And what's number two?"

"Number two?"

"You said there were two important things."

"Yes," Crash said. "Number two is you are really screwing us up."

"Who?"

"Me. The paper."

"Lawrence Dracut?"

"I see you have your own sources of information," Crash said.

Yes, I thought, the same Joan Bentley who had told him about me suspecting murder had told me about Lawrence Dracut taking over the *Patriot*.

"The thing is," Crash said, "if you start telling people that Molly Collins was murdered, you're going to screw up something we're trying to do here. Something big."

"What?"

"I can't tell you," Crash said. "But I can tell you I've been thinking about you and I can see some big benefits for you in this."

"Just like the old days," I said wryly.

"Right, just like the old days."

In the old days, in Florida, Crash had a lot of small,

unsophisticated clients, and one night at the dog track he had suggested that I write articles about his clients and he would pay me double what I was getting from the magazine or newspaper. My editors would print my stories because they trusted me, and they wouldn't know I was feeding them puffery. The whole thing was unethical as hell, but I said, sure, Crash, great idea. I'd get maybe a hundred or so from the magazine, but then Crash would bill the client two grand for the exposure, and slip me an extra two hundred. Crash and I had always gotten along well because we were about equally corrupt. "Big benefits," Crash was saying now, "but you've got to cool it with this 'Molly was murdered' crap."

"Just tell me one thing," I said.

"What?"

"If I keep asking questions about Molly's accident, am I in any danger?"

"Danger? Shit, no," Crash said. "What do you think, I'm trying to protect some murderer? Jesus, Scotty, give me some credit, huh? I'm not that slimy. I'm telling you the truth, I've got no reason to believe that Molly was murdered. And I'm leveling with you when I say that if you keep quiet it could mean big benefits for you. Possibly some very serious bucks."

"And that's all you can tell me?"

"That's it."

I believed Crash. What we had done together was a bit shady, but he had always treated me fairly.

A promise of silence would be no great sacrifice for me, anyhow. Joan had told Crash and God knows who else. If I didn't stop yapping to other people about my suspicion, the whole world would soon know, including the murderer. Not desiring to have my throat slit again, I decided it would be best to keep my mouth shut.

"Look, Crash," I said, "I can't promise that I'll give up on this Molly thing, but I'll tell you what, I won't speak to anybody else about it, okay?"

"Good man," Crash said. "You won't be sorry."

CHAPTER 4

Later that week I went to see Lillian Gilmartin at the *Boston Times,* which is housed in an aging, gothic sort of building in Post Office Square. I had charmed the editor of *Boston Magazine* into giving me an assignment to interview Lillian Gilmartin. I did not tell him that I wanted to interview "Luv, Lilly," so that I could dig for clues to Molly's murder.

The newsroom at the *Times* was big enough for a Frisbee tournament. This is what it would be like if I had a job, I thought as I weaved my way past the desks of wizened reporters who jabbed at keyboards and shouted important journalistic questions like, "Hal, what's the point spread on the Celtics's game?"

Someone pretty directed me to Lillian's desk. I approached Lillian from behind. She was staring into an ornate little compact and dabbing on face powder. Her desk was a mess.

"Lillian Gilmartin?" I said.

Lillian put away her compact mirror and swiveled around from her video terminal, which displayed the first draft of the next "Luv, Lilly" column.

"Geez," Lillian said, "you caught me making myself beeoootiful."

It was midday but she wore a powder-blue silk dress, more suitable for an evening at the Shubert, a fake pearl necklace, and more rings than she had fingers. Now in her early sixties, Lillian wore makeup mainly as camouflage. Her famous strawberry-blond hair, rapidly turning gray, was curled and still shiny. Could this person have killed my Molly? I wondered.

I put out a hand for Lillian to shake. "Jeff Scotland," I explained.

Her own hand, fleshy and pink, squeezed mine demurely. She smiled, her cheeks bobbing on her face like two plums in a bowl of milk.

"The interview," I said.

"Well, sure, the interview," she said, flirtatiously slapping at me. "Geez, you didn't think I forgot, did you?"

"No," I said.

Lillian rose heavily from her swivel chair. "C'mon, let's talk in the lunchroom," she said, glancing disdainfully at the pale-faced men and women who surrounded her. "This is hardly the place to do an interview. All these morons listening to everything."

Carrying my briefcase, I followed Lillian out of the newsroom, along a poorly lighted corridor, down a flight of stairs, and into a long rectangle of a room that smelled exactly like the tin Davy Crockett lunch box that I always carried to school in the third grade. The room contained a dozen metal chairs set haphazardly at two lunch tables that were arranged in a T-shape under long fluorescent lights. Pages from the morning edition were scattered everywhere.

"You know, I'm really flattered you're doing a story,"

Lillian said. "Geez, I haven't had a story done on me in three years." She stood next to the long acrylic counter. At one end there was a sink, and at the other there was a microwave oven, a Mr. Coffee, and a small refrigerator.

"You want something to eat?" she asked.

"Coffee will be fine."

She poked around in the cupboards over the counter. From across the room I could hear her bracelets jangling. "Will there be photographs?" she asked, touching at her hair with those much bejeweled fingers.

"They'll send a photographer next week," I said.

"Fine," she said, "just as long as they give me plenty of notice, so I can make myself beeoootiful!"

I placed my briefcase on the table and pulled out my tape recorder and the index cards on which I had printed my questions for Lillian.

Lillian, hunched over now, with her head almost inside the refrigerator, looked more portly than the last time I had seen her, at Legal Sea Foods restaurant. Lillian was, well, a fat woman. So fat, in fact, that her obesity inspired derisive comments every time "Luv, Lilly" gave weight-loss advice in her column. However, the seeming contradiction of Lillian telling a reader in Malden to lose weight while Lillian was stout enough to sink a dinghy never troubled Lillian. Her argument was that you should lose weight if you want to, but she didn't want to. In fact, Lillian was an advocate for hefty women, and always managed to dress stylishly, if inappropriately, in clothes she got for free from Queenies, a Copley Place boutique that sold only to "the full-figured" woman. Large ladies everywhere loved Lilly.

Okay, so Lillian is fat, I thought. No crime in that. But is she also some kind of a psycho who will put a cake knife into my back the minute she finds out I'm on to her? I was beginning to feel ridiculous.

"You want some?" she said now, turning from the refrigerator and wiggling a red box at me.

"Huh?"

"Microwave pancakes," she explained, smiling proudly as if she had invented them. "Do you want some? They're quite tasty."

"No, thanks."

Lillian tore open the box, pulled three pancakes out of a plastic bag, and slid them into the microwave. "Well," she said as she jabbed a pudgy pink finger at the cooking controls, "what's the angle?"

"The angle?"

"On the story you're writing about me."

"Giving advice in the 1990s," I said.

"Great," she said. "I have a few thoughts about that."

I felt guilty because Lillian, in her euphoria over being interviewed, seemed so harmless. And here I was, accusing her—at least in my mind—of murder.

Tell me, Miss Gilmartin, I thought, our readers would like to know, did you hit my friend with a car?

"Let's go back a bit," I said. I turned on my tape recorder. The microwave buzzed. Lillian grabbed her plate of pancakes and coffee for us both. She sat down across from me and began eating her pancakes with a plastic fork.

"How long have you been giving advice?" I asked.

"I started when I was still a virgin," she said with a wink. "That should give you some idea."

Lillian was off and running. Most of what she told me I had already learned from my research at the Boston Public Library in Copley Square. There I had found a profile of Lillian that had been published in *New Eng-*

land Magazine, and *Yankee* had once included her in a roundup of New England women newspaper columnists. And there were dozens of smaller newspaper stories over the years. I had researched Lillian because I had learned, from writing true crime books, that when you are presented with a mystery in a person's present, you can often find a clue if you look closely at her past.

Lillian had grown up in Boston, lived near the trolley tracks in the Jamaica Plain section of the city. Even as a kid Lillian was fat. Taunted for her plumpness, she grew up tough, a real street kid, a devout Christian, a whiz at math, and, against all odds, a neighborhood roller-skating champion. After high school Lillian got a job as a waitress at Durgin Park. She socked away her tip money, applied for a couple of scholarships, and finally had enough bucks to enter Boston University. There she studied journalism until she dropped out to take care of her mother, who had become deranged. When her mother died, Lillian went to Cincinnati, where she bluffed her way into a job as a newspaper reporter. When the Ohio paper decided to run an advice column, they gave the job to Lillian.

"I was ecstatic. I felt as if I had found the thing that God had created me for," she said, finishing off her pancakes. "So I was writing an advice column even before the nitwit twins."

I knew who the nitwit twins were. Lillian's hostility toward Ann Landers and Ann's twin sister, Dear Abby, was well known.

"But they're in their seventies," I said.

"That's because they were thirty-seven before they even started," Lillian said, "and, Geez, neither one of them had a day's experience at anything relevant."

This was true. At the library I had learned that in 1955

most advice columns were written by local columnists, like Lillian. There were a few syndicated columns then, like the Dorothy Dix column and the Ann Landers column, which then was written by Ruth Montgomery, a journalist and registered nurse. When Ruth Montgomery died, her newspaper, the *Chicago Sun-Times,* needed a new woman to write the Ann Landers column. Eppie Lederer, the woman we now call Ann Landers, wasn't what anybody would call qualified for the job. But she had chutzpah and influential friends, and she beat out a slew of qualified applicants for the job. Within a year Eppie's twin sister, Popo, got a similar job with the *San Francisco Chronicle.* Popo called herself Abigail Van Buren and her column was known as "Dear Abby."

"A couple of vipers is what they are," Lillian said. "Those cows didn't know enough about writing or giving advice to fill a thimble. They were just lucky. They were a couple of society ladies who had friends in high places. They put a lot of good people out of work."

"How's that?"

"The nitwit twins were popular, God knows why. When they started syndicating—this was in '56—newspapers all over the country wanted to run Ann Landers or 'Dear Abby.' Well, sure, any newspaper's going to pay a few bucks for a syndicated column if they can fire someone who's getting a salary. So I was fired. Just like that. Out of a job because the paper had picked up 'Dear Abby,' a woman who had never been a journalist or a therapist or anything else that might remotely qualify her for the job. I was heartbroken. God, I could have beat Abby to death with a rake."

Could have killed her, huh, I thought. The way you killed Molly? It was a powerful admission. Only problem was, Lillian had not killed "Dear Abby."

"And her nitwit sister, too," Lillian was saying. "I could have strangled the two of them. Which is funny, when you think of it."

"How's that?"

Now Lillian was riled up. Her face was turning red. "Because around that time the two of them sisters could have strangled each other. Now, that really burns me. I mean people say, how can Lillian Gilmartin tell people to lose weight when she's so fat, herself? Well, what about the nitwit twins? Here they are, telling everybody in the world how to fix a relationship, and they can't even talk to each other for twenty years! Two experts on communication and neither one of them can talk to her own twin sister. Is that the height of irony or what? A couple of frauds, that's what they are, a couple of frauds. Think they're so fancy with their fur coats. Couple of frauds."

"You must have felt at some point that their success could have been yours," I said, probing.

"Who needs it?" Lillian said. "I never wanted all that. I just wanted my own advice column. And they took it away from me."

"What did you do then?"

"For ten years I worked as a reporter, first in Baltimore, then back here in Boston. Geez, it was great being home, being able to go to Fenway Park again. In 1966 I married Fred Lincoln. A dentist. He's dead. We had three kids, so I dropped out of journalism. I baked cookies, washed floors, all that housewifey stuff." She leaned across the table, smacked my arm playfully, and smiled with great glee. "At least until I got poooolitical," she said. "What a riot, huh? Me, in politics."

In the early 1970s, when the school bussing issue came along and fractured the city, Lillian ran for the Boston School Committee. Her booming voice, and atrocious grammar (which had never shown up in her writing), were, in that strange political climate, assets. To the great unwashed she was just plain Lilly, and for that they rewarded her with a seat on the committee.

Lillian was a vocal, some say fanatical, opponent of forced bussing to achieve integration. They adored her in Southie and Charlestown. She once chained herself to a post in front of city hall. Another time she lay down on the street to stop a bus that was transporting white kids to a previously all-black school in Roxbury. People accused her of leaving dead animals on the mayor's doorstep. It just made her more popular. Her motto, carried on banners by a thousand distressed mothers: THEY CAN'T DO THIS TO US.

After one term Lillian Gilmartin abandoned the School Committee and, now with a locally famous name, went looking for a new job in journalism. What she really wanted, she let it be known, was a job as an advice columnist. The *Patriot,* which had no syndicated advice column, scooped her up. Certainly her sometimes rude manners and dumb-as-a-fox street style of dealing with people did not fit perfectly into the *Patriot's* respectable image, but she wrote well enough, and they knew that "Luv, Lilly" would woo some blue-collar readers from the equally respectable *Boston Times* and the tabloid *Record American.* DEAR LILLY CARES ABOUT BOSTON trumpeted the billboards on MBTA buses when she arrived, a provincial slap at the other papers, which carried Chicago-based syndicated columns.

Lillian Gilmartin's advice came in two colors. Black and white. Abortion was wrong, period. Premarital sex was immoral, end of discussion. America was good, no debate. All murderers, rapists, and child molesters should hang, all marriages could be saved, except the ones where the husband was a wife-beater, and any woman who was dumb enough to stick with a wife-beater shouldn't come whining to "Luv, Lilly" about it. All of the problems of American life were boiled down into simple syrup by "Luv, Lilly" years before Ronald Reagan mastered the recipe.

Despite an inability to perceive complexity in human relationships, a failing which made syndication of "Luv, Lilly" unthinkable, Lillian caught on. Her bluntness and her childlike certainty about right and wrong were reassuring to her fans, and amusing to her detractors. The *Patriot*'s circulation rose dramatically.

"I was the most popular columnist they had," Lillian said. "I was getting three thousand letters a week."

It was true. But the newspaper industry was changing. By the end of the 1970s many suburban newspapers, like the *Bay State News*, were draining subscribers and advertising bucks from the big city dailies. The *Bay State News*, with its color pictures, slick graphics, and state-of-the-art printing plant, was outselling all Boston papers in a dozen Middlesex County communities west of the city. One big reason for *BSN*'s success was its popular advice columnist, a hip, bright, and compassionate young woman named Molly Collins. "Dear Molly."

"God, you would have thought she was Joan of Arc, or somebody, the way they carried on," Lillian said when I cautiously steered us around to the subject of Molly. "The *Patriot* was convinced all they had to do was hire Molly and they would boost their circulation and destroy the *Bay State News*. So they offered her disgusting amounts of money, and then they had to syndicate her to get it back."

"So you left."

"They fired me, honey. Let's call it what it was. They

made me a scapegoat, that's what. You know what a scapegoat is? That's what I was. Circulation's off, let's fire Lillian. I got pushed out of my dream for the second time. I couldn't believe it was happening all over again. I had just lost my husband and now my life's work was being taken away from me. I had a nervous breakdown after that. Spent four months in a retreat up in New Hampshire. That's what they called it, a retreat. When I was a kid we would have called it a nut house. I was inconsolable."

"And that's why you hated Molly Collins?" I said. Now we were getting to it.

"Look," Lillian said. "I wouldn't speak ill of the dead in any case. But the truth is that stuff about a feud between Molly and me was strictly showbiz. After I got the advice column job here at the *Times,* the know-it-alls in publicity figured it would help everybody if we could claim there was a feud between Molly and me. You know, we did all those 'Good Day' shows together, answering the same letters in our very different ways."

"But you never talked to her, even on TV."

"She never talked to me, either. If you want to know the truth, I think Molly hated me. Probably felt guilty or something because of what she done to me."

"What she did to you?"

"Yeah, taking my job."

"And you made nasty comments about her."

"It was all an act," Lillian said. "They said it would sell papers."

"I see. And you never resented it when she became rich and famous, just the way Ann and Abby had."

"Not at all. I could have had all that anytime I wanted. Lots of syndicates wanted me, lots of them. I didn't need all that."

Now what, Scotty? I thought. What's your next question? Did you kill her, Lilly? Did you smash her down with your car? And why? I felt like a man who had come upon a bear in the woods and had no bullets in his rifle. I didn't have a witness, a secret photograph, a damning bit of evidence, something I could thrust in front of Lillian's jowly face and say, "How do you explain this?" There was to be no "Aha!," no satisfaction. All I had was a pleasant enough woman who might or might not have hated Molly for something that happened years ago. I guess I'd known all along that Lillian was an unlikely suspect. But, sadly, I had no others.

I spent the rest of the interview asking Lillian about advice-giving in the 1990s, the very thing I had supposedly come for. Her basic message: nothing's changed. Good advice in 1955 was good advice today. As we talked, I tried not to hate her for the catty things she had said about Molly. Maybe it all really was just showbiz.

When we were done, I put the tape recorder away. I rose uneasily, thinking maybe there was one final question I could ask that would put this insane idea of mine to rest. But there wasn't. Lillian rose, too. She patted down her dress and fussed with her hair. Then the plum cheeks rose in a forced, nervous smile.

"Tell me," she said, "you don't seriously think that I murdered Molly Collins, do you?"

I was struck wordless for several seconds. I actually blushed, as if I had gotten caught in some lie.

"Huh? Who said that?"

"Joan Bentley," she said. "Molly's secretary."

"I didn't know you knew Joan."

"Of course, dear. Joan and I are good friends. I had to talk to her many times during the so-called feud. Whenever Molly and I were supposed to coordinate some public appearance, poor Joan had to be the go-between."

"So Molly and you wouldn't have to talk to each other."

"Exactly," Lillian said, and then, "I'm sorry. I've embarrassed you."

She didn't wait for an answer to her question. We walked back to her desk in the newsroom, and she showed me photos of her kids, now all grown and doing well. She gave me a hug as we said goodbye.

In the parking lot I searched with great diligence for Lillian's reserved parking spot, as if I might find her car splattered with Molly's blood and dented at the point of impact. Right, Scotty, I thought, and maybe there will be a note that says, "I killed Molly Collins. Luv, Lilly." When I found the Gilmartin slot, I made a note of the fact that Lillian drove a 1988 white Oldsmobile. I wrote down the registration number.

I drove back up I-93 feeling oddly relieved. If Lillian was not a suspect, then I had no leads. And if I had no leads, then nobody, including me, could reasonably expect me to investigate. I wanted to give up this "Molly was murdered crap," as Crash Galovitch had put it, and go back to being an utter failure.

When I got to Plum Island, Mungus was in T-Shirt Heaven, pressing the words YOU ARE NEVER ALONE WITH SCHIZOPHRENIA on a sweatshirt. Puffing on a cigarillo, he wore his Greek fisherman's cap and a sweatshirt that said DON'T ASK ME FOR ONE LIKE THIS. The customer, a bug-eyed young man, stood impatiently at the counter, shifting his weight from foot to foot as if he were purchasing condoms.

"Did you do it?" Mungus asked, after the customer left.

"Do what?"

"Tell Joan Bentley that you're a shallow human being, that you have no honorable intentions with her."

"Not yet," I said.

"Didn't think so."

"Besides, I wasn't with Joan. I was interviewing Lillian Gilmartin."

"Oh. Did she sign a confession?"

"No," I said.

I went to my office, and a few minutes later Mungus strolled through on his way to the shower. A towel was slung over his shoulder and he held a can of shaving cream in his hand. He was grooming for an afternoon date with a woman he had met at a bowling alley in Haverhill.

"I made over six thousand dollars in prizes today on *The Price Is Right*," he said proudly. "Plus, I'm going to Puerto Rico. I won an all-expenses-paid trip, six fabulous days and nights, taxes and all gratuities included. And a six-week supply of Bacon Bits."

Mungus watched a lot of game shows during the day and he likes to keep track of how he would have done if he had really been on the show playing the game.

"Great," I said. "Have a good trip."

"Oh, by the way, Tom Brady called," Mungus said. "Wants you to take over a magazine assignment for him. Can you do it?"

Does the Pope shit in the woods, I thought. Sure I could take over an assignment.

Poverty had been on my mind a lot lately. In fact, my larder had gotten so low that I was considering the most desperate of acts: getting a real job. On top of everything else, I would soon have to pay a divorce lawyer. Why, I wondered, couldn't civilized, childless Americans like Anne and me simply jump over a stick to get married and jump back over the stick to get divorced?

"Yes, I can take the assignment," I said. "Brady must be doing okay for himself if he can turn over assignments to utter failures like me."

"No," Mungus said. "He can't do it because he took a job."

"A job?"

"Digital," Mungus said, as if he were announcing the cause of death. "Staff writing job. He'll be writing training manuals and explaining to college graduates how to stick plug A into socket B."

"But he's written for *Rolling Stone* . . . *TV Guide*."

"Doesn't matter," Mungus said. "He says he can't make a living at it. He's bailing out."

"I can't believe it," I said to Mungus. "Brady is only thirty-five."

"Digital gets everybody," Mungus said, patting my back thoughtfully as he left the room. Digital Equipment Corporation, as near as I can figure out, had, at one time, employed everybody in Massachusetts who didn't do telemarketing or sell real estate.

"Well, they're not getting me," I said to the walls.

I called Brady at the *Worcester Telegram,* where he worked two days a week as a society columnist, an unusual job for a man who grows his own marijuana and writes porno under the name Guy Palmer. Brady had once told me he liked the society beat because it gave him a chance to meet rich young single women.

On the phone Brady was strangely buoyant for a man who would soon be drawing a salary. "Last day on the

beat," he said cheerfully. "If I don't meet Miss Wonderful by sundown, DEC owns my soul."

We talked for a while about the article assignment.
Then the weather, the latest films, the Bruins, the Celtics,
everything except the two tragedies that had invaded my
life since our last conversation.

Finally Brady chuckled. "So, I understand you're a
wild bachelor again," he said, putting the best possible
slant on the fact that I had been dropped from a plane
without a parachute.

"Yes," I said.

"Look, Scotty," he said, "I was real sad to hear about
Molly. I know you were close. Terrible thing. It was kind
of spooky, getting a party invitation from her the day
after she died."

I couldn't believe what I was hearing. "What did you
say?"

"I said I got an invitation from Molly. For a party. It
came the day after she died."

"She invited you to the party?" My heart was pounding.

"Yes."

"But you didn't know Molly."

"I only met her once, at a writer's union meeting."

"But you didn't really know her?"

"No," he said. "I was surprised that she invited me to
her party."

"She had your address?"

"No," he said. "She sent the invite to me here at the
Telegram."

"I see," I said. I could feel the old investigative juices
flowing again. I didn't know what was going on, and if
I had any sense I would leave it alone. But now I was
sure that Molly had been murdered, and I couldn't stop

myself. I'd been too much of a loser lately. I wanted to do one thing right. Screw Anne, I thought. And screw her new boyfriend. And screw the son of a bitch who killed my Molly.

After I said goodbye to Brady, I called Joan at the *Patriot*. In the back of my mind I could hear Fred McHale sharpening his knife.

CHAPTER 5

"Did you bring the list?" I asked Joan.

On the phone I had asked Joan to meet me for lunch and bring the invitation list for Molly's party. Now we sat at a table in the glass-enclosed rear section of Nooshie's in Quincy Market.

Joan looked hurt. "Yes," she said.

Then I realized that I hadn't said hello or how are you, or kissed her. I was so anxious to get my hands on the invitation list that I was letting my manners slip.

Joan tugged a kraft envelope out of her pocketbook and handed it to me. "What's so important about the invitation list?"

"I'll know in a minute," I said, grabbing at the envelope. And then, realizing that I was being unkind to a woman I cared about, I pushed the envelope aside. "Sorry," I said. "It can wait. How's everything at home?"

Joan brightened. Things at home were not entirely good, she said. She had a problem, and she thought I was the one who could give her good advice. Her wayward nephew, who was staying with her, had invited his sister and the sister's lowlife husband to camp at Joan's house while the three of them straightened out their lives, which, I gathered, was something they did at least three times a year. The nephew hadn't troubled Joan or her husband for permission before extending his invitation, and now the adventurous couple was driving up from Florida in an unregistered Toyota. Joan told me the story in elaborate detail. I listened, but all the time my fingers ached to open the envelope.

"I haven't got room for these people," Joan said. She sounded desperate. "But I can't just put people out on the street. What would you do?"

"Give them two weeks to make other plans," I said, glancing anxiously at the envelope. "It will be uncomfortable, but otherwise you'll feel like a crumb for throwing them out. And while they are in your house, make them sleep in your nephew's room. That will make him think twice about inviting people to stay with you."

Joan liked the advice.

"And make them do the dusting and the vacuuming," I added.

We ordered lunch. I opened the envelope.

"I still don't understand why you want the invitation list," Joan said.

"Look, Joan, I'd like to tell you what this is all about, but I can't have everybody in New England knowing that I think Molly was murdered."

Joan looked as if she'd been slapped in the face.

"You think I'd tell?"

"You told Lillian Gilmartin that I suspected her," I said.

Joan blushed. "Lillian told you?"

"Yes," I said. "I must admit she took it very well. And just for the record, I doubt that she's the killer, though it did occur to me that an automobile is the perfect murder weapon for an overweight recognizable female."

"I'm sorry," Joan said. "But I just didn't take it seriously. It was like a joke. We were chatting on the phone and it just came out, 'Hey, Jeff Scotland thinks you murdered Molly Collins.' It was such an absurd idea."

"Right," I said. "Absurd. And you told Crash Galovitch."

Joan seemed to sink in her chair. "I'm sorry," she said.

"Forget it," I said, "it's over." There was an artificial yellow rose on every table. I plucked ours from its vase and handed it to Joan as a peace offering.

I pulled out the long, neatly typed list of people who had been invited to Molly's party, and began scanning for names that would fit my theory. Allan Hirting from WBZ was on the list. Jean Dosantos from the *Boston Phoenix* was on the list. Randy Freidus from Channel 56 was also on the list. I read these names to Joan.

"So?" she said. "I don't get it. There are a lot of media people on the list."

"Yes, but my friend Tom Brady at the *Worcester Telegram* was also invited, and these people have something in common with him."

"What?"

"None of them were friends of Molly."

"No?"

"They were invited because they were media people."

"I don't understand," Joan said.

"I think Molly was going to announce something at the party," I said. "Something newsworthy."

That was it. I sat across from Joan, perhaps seeming calm, but inside I was more furious than I had ever been. Molly was going to announce something and somebody stopped her. If I knew what it was, then maybe I could figure out why she was killed.

"I'm scared," Joan said. "This idea of Molly being murdered. It's starting to seem real."

Later that afternoon, when Joan and I were making love at the Arlington Day's Inn, I thought I could feel the fear eddying through her body. Or maybe it was my own body, my own fear. Maybe there was good reason to be afraid. What if I did figure out what Molly was going to announce? What if I did guess who killed her? Then what? Did I really want to know?

Joan and I made love for a long time, pretending for a few precious hours that there was no husband, no kid, and that nobody's heart was going to be broken. Later we took a bubble bath. Even in the bathtub she clung to her make-believe rose, and she tickled my nose with it.

Submerged in warm water and Mr. Bubble, we talked about our marriages. I had this new theory that first marriages don't work. Anne and I had been friends and lovers, and then the whole thing had expired like a library card, I said. Joan said that her husband had been great at first, too, but as he became more successful, he and Joan had gone less often to canoe on the Merrimac River, had seen fewer movies, had made less love. She still loved him, she guessed, but it all seemed hollow.

"He hardly knows I exist," she said. She put her rose aside and built little castles with the bubbles. "I almost told him about you. Crazy, huh?"

"Very," I said.

"I guess I just wanted to make him jealous. Anyhow, I didn't tell. Because I didn't want to ruin what we've got."

After Joan and I kissed goodbye in front of the motel, I drove back to Boston. I needed to see Molly's office again. I told myself I would search her office for some clue to what her announcement was going to be. But it was more than that. Except for one heartbreaking day when I'd helped Molly's sister empty Molly's apartment, I had steered clear of Molly things and Molly places. I'd been hiding from the very thing I needed, proof that Molly had lived, that our friendship had glowed as brightly as I remembered it. I knew that at least one more time I needed to be in space that she had occupied.

Route 2 was a rush-hour mess. I kept my eyes glued to the Hancock Tower in the distance so that I would not be thrown off in some wrong direction at a rotary and get lost, the way I often did. The crawl of traffic gave me plenty of time to think. I was troubled by how easily my mind could be seduced from thoughts of Molly's murder to thoughts of Joan. "Commitment," my wife had once said, "is not your strong suit." Perhaps, I thought now, but Anne, you're the one who left.

Besides, I told myself, investigating Molly's murder didn't mean I had to check into a monastery. There was no reason I couldn't work on the case and have a love affair with Joan at the same time. The case. That's how I had always thought of my stories when I was a true crime writer. I called them cases, as if I were some kind of detective. It made me more colorful at parties.

I got to Boston at five in the afternoon, and for an absurd amount of money I was allowed to park on the highest level of an indoor lot in Park Square. I walked the few blocks to the *Patriot*, which was on a slummy little street behind the theater district, housed in a narrow brownstone building that had been built when Herbert

Hoover was president. Boston has the best old buildings west of Europe, and though this one was neither unique nor notable, I would not trade it for a dozen glass towers.

I took the elevator up to the fourth floor. Molly's office was one of three private offices that had been constructed at one end of a clattering fluorescent newsroom. Like trailers for movie stars, the three offices had been installed as perks for the *Patriot*'s three writing stars, their syndicated columnists: Molly, the advice columnist; Brem Hyde, the political columnist; and Eric Elfin, the astrologer.

I walked invisibly through the busy newsroom. When I got to the back, I tried the doorknob to Molly's office. The door was locked. I didn't know what I thought I would do inside, anyhow. I peered through the glass on the door, squinted really, as if that would help me to see something that wasn't there.

The memories descended on me. There had been a time when I would frequently come to this office to meet Molly for lunch. I had spent long hours in the office because if Molly happened to be in the middle of someone's problem, she would refuse to leave. "But, Molly," I would say, "we're talking about hot pastrami on pumpernickel with mustard, and roast beef, cut thin as paper. And coffee that comes from a pot, not a machine." But you couldn't bribe Molly. She always had to answer the letter first, as if the poor shnook who'd sent it was waiting outside the door for her answer. So I would perch myself on the edge of her desk and drink the swilly coffee from the vending machine, and Molly would explain to me exactly what was bugging "Depressed in Dayton" or "Left Out in Louisville." Together we would work out advice that was both satisfactory to the letter writer and entertaining to the millions of newspaper readers who would be eavesdropping. Then Molly and I would go off to lunch at Ken's Deli or Jacob Worth's, where Molly would squeeze my hand across the table and unload her own troubles, most of which involved members of my own sex who had turned out to be scum.

Now, as I stared through the glass on Molly's office door, trying to hold back tears, I saw that little had changed. The office was a hole that should have been filled by her presence, but the pink and green decor that Molly loved was the same. The desk near the front, where Joan used to sit, was bare and lifeless. But on Molly's desk there were still books and pens and a small makeup mirror, left undisturbed, as if she were coming back. They were trivial items, now made poignant by her absence. The big electric typewriter, which I had hauled up from a storeroom when Molly went berserk on computers, was still plugged in. At the back of the office were four deep cartons, filled with unanswered letters. The cartons had always been there. In addition to Joan, Molly had four helpers in another part of the building, whose sole job was to pull letters out of those boxes, turn over the best ones to Molly, and answer the rest. Molly had insisted that every letter be answered, though a personal reply was not possible for each of the 25,000 advice seekers who wrote to her every week. Form letters were sent. One letter for alcohol problems. Another for people contemplating divorce. There was even an all-purpose inspirational letter for people whose problems didn't fit one of the other prewritten letters. These letters went out, along with the names and numbers of organizations that could help. Often Molly would scribble a personal note at the bottom of a letter.

Suddenly a voice behind me said, "It's sad to think of all those people who will never hear from Molly."

I turned. It was Brem Hyde, who had come from his office next door. "I thought I heard somebody skulking around out here," he said. We shook hands. I was embarrassed about my tears, but Brem didn't comment. "Come into my office and talk for a minute," Brem said. "We may not see each other for a while."

I put my fingers to my lips, kissed them, then pressed the kiss to the glass on Molly's door. We may not see each other for a while, I thought.

"A fucking tragedy," Brem said when we got into his office. I took his swivel chair. Brem lit his pipe and paced. It was an old ritual with us. Often, when Molly was driving me nuts, I would go into Brem's office while I waited for her. I would spin boyishly in the chair, and Brem, who hated to sit down, would pace and excoriate Jesse Helms and a number of other learning disabled senators.

Now Brem's office was almost bare. His Michael Jordan poster was gone and so was the photo of his three daughters that always sat on a shelf above his word processor. It made me think of Joan's kid and what would happen to him if she left her husband. Only a dictionary and an AP stylebook remained on Brem's bookshelf. Even his desk had that neat, carefully arranged look that is created by someone who's just marking time.

"What's going on? Looks like you're having a yard sale here."

"I'm leaving," he said.

"Leaving? You mean the *Patriot*?"

"Yes."

"Why leave the *Patriot*?" I said. "You've got a racket here. You sit around jerking off in your office all day and type three columns a week. What do they take you, an hour each?"

"About that," Brem said. We both knew that a good column could take several days. "Got a better offer. *San Francisco Chronicle*."

"Just like that, they called you up?"

"No," Brem said. "I went looking."

"But I thought you loved Boston. Who are you going to root for, the Golden State Warriors? The Sacramento Kings? Brem, this is serious."

"I'll always be a Celtics fan," he said.

"Then why go?"

"Lawrence Dracut," he said.

"Then it's true. He's buying the paper."

"Already bought it," Brem said. "I don't want to work for him. The guy's a carpetbagger. He'll be in here running the paper before long."

Brem Hyde was one of the last left-wingers, and it infuriated him that Dracut buried stories about labor unions, affirmative action, and the environment. Dracut, a libertarian, was often mistaken for a right-winger, especially by lefties.

"This is kind of sudden, isn't it?" I said.

"Not so sudden. The scumbucket came to an agreement six months ago, but he had to unload a radio station before he could officially own a newspaper in the same market. FCC regulations."

Affirmative action, I thought suddenly. The environment. Journalistic integrity. Do these things sound familiar, Scotty? They should. Molly was passionate about all of them. Of course. She had left a clue behind. Her principles. Molly would never have worked for Lawrence Dracut. Never. She would have quit just like Brem. I was sure of it. That's what she was going to announce at her party. But it still didn't make sense. You don't kill a woman just because she's going to quit her job.

"So Dracut overpaid for the *Patriot*," I said. I wanted to spill all my thoughts out to Brem, but I had promised Crash Galovitch I would tell nobody.

"How's that?"

"Well, he bought a paper that had a nationally syndicated advice columnist and a nationally syndicated political columnist. You and Molly were bringing in a lot of bucks to the *Patriot*. Now you're both gone."

I didn't even know what I was getting at, but I felt as if I had strayed at least into the killer's backyard.

"Don't worry about Lawrence Dracut," Brem said. "He'll make the best of things. He always does."

CHAPTER 6

"Angina?" I said to Dr. Lewis five weeks later. "You're telling me I've got angina?"

My heart was pounding. The humiliating examination of my naked body was over and now we sat, fully clothed, in his narrow office, with his desk between us. I could feel sweat forming on my hands.

Dr. Jack Lewis looked at me strangely. "Not angina. I said reflux. Reflux."

"Oh. It sounded like angina."

"Reflux sounded like angina?" he asked, frowning.

"I guess I'm just tense," I said. "What the Christ is reflux?"

"Reflux esophagitis," he said proudly. "It's a digestive problem. If I could show you a picture of your esophagus, you would think it was Mount St. Helens. When you lie down at night, your stomach dumps acid back into the esophagus. That's why you have that discomfort in your chest that you always think is a heart attack."

I felt a momentary sense of relief. I wasn't dying, after all, but then I remembered how often I pick up *USA Today* and discover that doctors have been wrong all along about something or other. The apprehension began to rise in me again.

I was in Dr. Lewis's office because I had become terrified about my health. My heart seemed to beat too often. My fingers trembled over the keyboard on my word processor. And often I felt as if a load of laundry had been stuffed into my chest cavity. I had pretty much worn out the self-diagnosis symptom chart in my home medical encyclopedia, so Lewis seemed to be my only recourse.

The breakup of my marriage and Molly's death had made me a physical wreck. Plus, at no extra charge, every time I looked into a mirror I saw the face of a man who was falling in love with a woman he could never have, and a coward who was backing away from investigating his friend's probable murder just because he didn't want to have his throat sliced open like a beefsteak tomato. It was February. My credit cards were maxed out. Article assignments were getting harder to come by. And my investigation of Molly's death was beginning to feel like a memory. The only sleuthing I'd done in two months was the relatively safe mission of tracking down the four witnesses to the accident. They all agreed that Molly had been hit by a black or blue or white, or possibly red, Buick, Mazda, sports car, or, as one of them put it, "one of those European cars, what do you call them?" None of the witnesses had gotten a good look at the driver.

Jack Lewis's brown eyes sparkled, as they always did when he talked about disease. He was a handsome fellow. I'd known him for five years and had noticed that he was one of those rats who get better looking as they get older. I couldn't help wondering if anything disgusting had happened in his office that day, but I wasn't in a mood to ask. He smiled. He seemed especially delighted to describe to me the lower esophageal sphincter. Drawing pictures in the air with his long fingers, he explained the ways in which my sphincter was malfunctioning. Then he stared down at my entire medical history, which was spread out on his desk, much the way I imagine a coroner's report would be.

There was a long silence while he read, now and then murmuring meaningfully and tapping his silky brown mustache. If I had still been with Anne at the time, I would have suspected that he was going to call my wife in later and tell her, "Look, Anne, Scotty is dying from one of the worst things I have ever seen. I only told him it was reflux so he wouldn't make a scene in the office. But, frankly, he's doomed." However, since my only contact with Anne since October had been through her lawyer, and since I had no close relatives that Dr. Lewis could shock with the news, I concluded that he was telling the truth.

"What's the cure?" I asked.

Lewis looked up. "Put some six-inch wooden blocks under the head of your bed," he said. "That will keep the acids from pouring back into your esophagus."

"That's all? A little carpentry and I'm cured?"

Lewis shook his head. "No more caffeine or alcohol," he said.

"Christ."

"Or chocolate," he said. "No tea, no onions, no garlic."

"Anything else?"

"No peppermint. No orange juice, no lemon juice, no tomato juice, that sort of thing."

"That sort of thing? You mean food."

"I've got a list," he said. From the top drawer of his

desk he took out a prescription pad and a list of the never-to-be-eaten.

"What's going on, Doc?" I said. "I never had to worry about things like my esophagus before."

"You were never middle-aged before."

"Middle-aged. You make it sound like a tumor. Is that what causes reflux? Being middle-aged?"

"Stress causes it," he said. "Is there something worrying you?"

"I'm worried about getting shot by a jealous husband," I said.

"Why? Who have you been humping?"

Lewis did not smile. To him, "Who have you been humping?" was just a routine medical question, like "Have you noticed any blood in your stool lately?"

Before I could answer, Lewis turned his head from me and stared at the wall on which his medical certificates hung, all neatly framed and carefully spaced. He stared at me for a moment. His eyes shifted and I could tell that my medical problems were boring him.

"So," he said, smiling now, "who do you think will be the new Molly Collins?"

"Huh?"

"Molly Collins, the advice columnist. She was a friend of yours, wasn't she?"

"Yes," I said. It still startled me to hear Molly talked about in the past tense.

"So, what sort of person do you think they'll choose to replace her?"

What the hell does this have to do with my heart palpitations and the fire in my guts? I wondered.

"I don't think they will replace her," I said.

"It's in the paper," Lewis said. "The contest."

"Contest?"

"Sure. Didn't you see the *Patriot* this morning?" He grabbed the newspaper from his desk and waved it at me. "It's on the front page. They're having a nationwide search to find the new Molly Collins. You just write them a letter and tell them why you should be the next 'Dear Molly.' They even took out a full page ad in *USA Today*. Anybody can apply. Butchers, bakers, candlestick makers." He stared at his diplomas. "Doctors," he said. Then, "Tell me honestly, do you think I'd be good at that?"

"Sure," I said. Really, I had no idea. But if I said no, he might overlook a cancer in my rectum someday. A contest, I thought.

Now I knew why Crash Galovitch had asked me to stop snooping. Whispers of murder would not have been the best PR for this nationwide contest. A contest to replace Molly. What a bizarre idea. I'd always thought of Molly as irreplaceable.

"The reason I thought of the 'Dear Molly' thing," Lewis went on, "is that you are obviously under a great deal of stress, and I imagine having your friend die like that is a big part of it."

"It didn't help," I said.

With that, there was a shriek from down the hallway. Lewis stood up. "Excuse me for a moment," he said. "It sounds as if my nurse is murdering another patient."

Stress, I thought. Is that all that's wrong with me? Was that the name for this great malaise which had set in like an abscessed tooth right after Anne's departure and Molly's death? Is that what made me think that the whole world was on its deathbed? It seemed to me not just that my life was going poorly, but that there were more elderly couples being clubbed to death in their button shops, more crazed terrorists steering trucks into marine barracks, more treacherous industrialists dumping toxic chemicals into the nearest river than ever before. And, I thought sadly, more brain-dead drivers knocking down pedestrians like bowling pins as they stepped off the curb. In fact, I sometimes thought how plentiful crazed and reckless drivers were in the city, and would momentarily abandon the absurd and overly dramatic notion that my Molly had been murdered. But even then, when I could dismiss her message and the invitation list, as coincidence, I still had fantasies of capturing the hit-and-run driver who had killed Molly, and torturing him for days on end with chains and sticks in a remote mountain cabin. The whole world, including me, had gone crazy. And now they were having a contest to replace my dead friend. A contest. That had to be the craziest thing yet. Would this new person be required to call me up and ask how I was doing from time to time? Would they make her send me cute little Ziggy postcards that said "I miss you"? Would she have to bring me a giant Valentine every year the way Molly did? Get a grip on yourself, Scotty, I thought, you're slipping. I reached across Lewis's desk for the newspaper.

BOSTON—Lawrence Dracut, publisher and editor of the *Boston Patriot*, has announced that a contest will be held to find a replacement for the nationally syndicated advice columnist Molly Collins. Collins, who was known all over the world for her "Dear Molly," column, died in October after being hit by an automobile.

"We're looking for someone with wit, good writing skills, common sense, and good advice," Dracut said yesterday at a press conference held to announce the contest. "The competition is open to everybody. We're not looking just for journalists and therapists. There are millions of ordinary people out there with good advice to give, and we want to hear from them.

"To enter the contest all you have to do is send us a letter and tell us why you should be the next Molly Collins, and include a photograph of yourself," Dracut said.

According to Joseph Galovitch, director of public relations for the *Patriot*, the most qualified applicants will be asked to answer simple letters. "The responses," said Galovitch, "will be judged by a panel of experts consisting of clergymen, psychologists, and journalists. But the final decision will be made by Lawrence Dracut and selected members of the newspaper staff."

A few minutes later Dr. Lewis came back into the office. "Some people are just not good with needles," he explained. He sat behind his desk again and stared at my medical records. My mind was still on the newspaper story, and it occurred to me that the winner of the contest would have a pretty good motive for killing Molly, but only if she knew in advance that there would be a contest and that she would win it. In other words, my idea didn't make any sense at all.

"So what else is causing stress?" Lewis said. "The divorce?"

"Sure, the divorce," I said. "And money. Kids with guns. Air pollution. Apartheid."

"What have you got, a list or something?"

"And a woman," I said.

"Because she's married?" he said, leaning forward for details.

"Yes," I said. "To a doctor."

Lewis glanced at his phone. Perhaps he was thinking of calling home.

"Well," he said, "that can be very stressful, wondering if the husband is going to catch you in the sack and cut your testicles off with a scalpel."

"Yes," I said, crossing my legs.

Lewis glanced at his watch. Apparently my reference to adultery had reminded him of his next patient. He leaned back in his swivel chair and stared for a moment at the ceiling.

"Dear Dr. Lewis," he said, running one hand slowly through the air, as if he were setting the words in type.

"Huh?"

" 'Dear Dr. Lewis.' How would that be for the title of an advice column?"

"Okay, I guess."

"Don't you think a doctor would have an edge in the contest?" he said. "I mean, what does a plumber know about dealing with human problems?"

I told Lewis he was right, a doctor would have an edge. Actually, I was annoyed. I was forever running into doctors who thought they could write for publication, though they would be appalled if I proposed to perform surgery.

"Anything else stressing you?" Lewis said. His tone of voice had changed. He had switched into advice columnist mode, and now he sounded like a late-night FM disc jockey.

"Sometimes I feel that if I knew where I could buy some explosives I'd go to New York and put an end to a few of the nation's top magazines," I said.

Dr. Lewis put up a hand. "That's the stress talking," he said. Lewis folded his hands in front of him on the desk.

He leaned forward and offered his wisest advice-columnist expression.

"Being a freelance writer is a stressful business," he said. "It's not like being a doctor where you know that people are going to become panic-stricken over some lump under their tongue and they have to come to you whether they can afford it or not. You're a writer, and there's always the chance that you will never make another cent."

"Thanks for the encouragement, Doc."

"That causes worry," he said, "and worry can kill you just as surely as a hypodermic full of air. You name a disease, and worriers get it. Heart attacks. Cancer. Ulcers. Diabetes. Brain embolism. Lung infections—"

"I get the point," I said.

"Rashes. Anxiety attacks. Hair loss . . ."

"What are you saying?" I asked.

"You want my advice?"

His smile was a mile wide. This was it, his debut as an advice columnist.

"Yes," I said. "I want your advice."

"My advice," he announced, "is that you should get a steady job with a regular paycheck. Freelancing is a young man's game."

Get a job? What was this guy, working for my ex-wife or something?

"You make it sound like I'm on Medicare," I said. "Besides, age is a state of mind."

"Yes, and I'm trying to tell you that your physical problems are being caused by your state of mind. You're grieving over a divorce. You've had a close friend die. You had that incident with the convict a few years back."

"That *incident* is what made me quit writing true crimes," I said.

I remembered now that Molly had tried to talk me out of quitting when she came to see me in the hospital. She had brought flowers, and all the nurses were so impressed that I actually knew *the* Molly Collins.

"It was more than an incident," I said to Dr. Lewis. "It was a major trauma."

"Yes, it was, and that's what I'm getting at," Lewis said. "There are several stress factors you can't control, so you've got to control the ones you can."

"Such as?"

"Such as 'Will I get a check in time to pay my bills or won't I?' Such as 'Will I get an assignment this week or won't I?' You're living the life of a victim. Everybody's got the power in your life except you. It's time to take some control over your life. Get a job and you'll get healthy."

He leaned back in his chair, folded his arms across his chest, smiled smugly.

"Dr. Jack has spoken," he said. "That reminds me, how do you think I should sign my letters? Dr. Jack, or Dr. Lewis? Or maybe, Jack Lewis, M.D.?"

"Why don't you worry about that after you've got the job," I suggested.

"You're right," he said. "There will probably be a lot of applicants."

"Job," I said. "What a frightful word." I guess I had known even before I walked into Lewis's office that I had come to the end of the line, freedom-wise. The box of unopened bills under my desk. The phone calls from collection agencies. The checks that came back marked "Returned for Insufficient Funds." There was a message in all of them. I would have to get a regular job.

Lewis stared at me for a long time. Is this the way he

stares at the ladies before he shoves his hand under their johnnies? I wondered.

"Get a job," he said. "And get yourself a girlfriend who is not married. That will cheer you up." He looked at his watch again. "I'll give you something for the reflux."

He scribbled something unreadable on the prescription pad.

"Take two of these a day," he said, handing me the prescription. "Watch your diet. If things don't get better by the time the bottle is empty, come back and see me and we'll shove a tube down your throat to see what's going on down there. Try to relax."

"How?"

"Meditate. Go to church if you have to."

I folded the prescription and put it in my pocket, wondering if I might be that one person in ten thousand who was allergic to this particular pharmaceutical product and would die in my sleep after taking it.

Lewis put his arm around me as we walked to the door.

"I truly am sorry about your friend," he said. "She was a great lady. The whole country loved her."

Yes, I thought. And so did I.

"Can I ask you something?" Lewis said.

"What's that?"

"Well, it's none of my business, but—"

"Go ahead," I said. "What is it?"

"Your friend, Molly Collins," he said.

"What about her?"

"How much money did she make a year?"

"Well, there was the syndication," I said.

"Uh-huh."

"And product endorsements."

"Uh-huh," Lewis said again. His eyes were enlarging.

"And the pamphlets that she sold through the mail, and her regular salary at the *Patriot*."

"Yes, yes," Lewis said. Now he was rubbing his hands together.

"And the speaking engagements, of course."

"Of course," Lewis said. He leaned close to me. He looked like he was about to drool.

"Over a million a year," I said.

"A million bucks a year," Lewis said. "Even a radiologist doesn't make that kind of money."

As I pulled out of the medical center parking lot and headed for home, I tried to get my mind on my work. I didn't want to think about Molly. It was the middle of a bad winter, and the snow piled by the sides of the road seemed now to be decaying. Everything else had a dreamlike quality about it.

Lewis was right, I thought. Stress was not my friend. Stress was chewing away at my esophagus. And who knew what would be next if I didn't get it under control. My pancreas? My gallbladder? My Cowper's gland, perhaps? I knew about the Cowper's gland because I had studied the male sex system for a satirical piece called "Why Men Are No Good," a piece which was turned down by all the best women's magazines. Anyhow, the point was that several of my lesser known glands had become a potential smorgasbord for stress-crazed stomach acids. I knew I had to do something to get my life under control.

The irony of this, I thought, was that for years I had been Mr. Cool, the unflappable Jeff Scotland, the last guy you'd expect to find in Walgreen's looking for a bargain price on a large jar of Rolaids. I was the one who was always telling people how to find peace, how to solve problems in their lives, how to get their emotions under control. People were always turning to me for advice. But things had changed. And now I was the one who had to settle down, get a job, end the affair with Joan, and give up coffee, or perish.

I was almost home when it occurred to me that there was one job I wouldn't mind having, a job that would give me the fame I had always craved, the money I had craved even more, and perhaps even the strength to let Joan go. Instead of investigating Molly's death, I could do something else for her, something safe. I could carry her torch. I could be the ultimate sensitive male. I could be the new Molly Collins.

CHAPTER 7

"The *Patriot* is having a contest to find the new Molly Collins," I said to Mungus.

We sat in a booth at the McDonald's in Newburyport. It was kids' video night or some such thing, and there were children hollering and romping while their mothers watched the *Sleeping Beauty* video that played on two televisions. Mungus had chosen this booth because from it he had an excellent view of a young mother who wore a low-cut blouse that showed cleavage every time she leaned over to put pieces of bread into her toddler's mouth.

"A contest to replace Molly?" Mungus said. One eyebrow went up.

"They're having a national search. Any bean brain can apply. I'm thinking of entering."

"You?" Mungus said. Both eyebrows went up.

"Sure, me. What's wrong with that?"

"It's funny," Mungus said.

"What's funny about it? I'm a writer. I wouldn't have to relocate. I was Molly's friend. I even helped her with letters. Who could be a more logical choice than me?"

Mungus looked at me the way you look at somebody who is deluding himself.

"Besides," I said, "I'm not the only one who thinks I'd have a shot. Crash Galovitch called this afternoon. He practically begged me to enter the contest."

"Now, there's a great judge of character," Mungus said. "Crash Galovitch. Hasn't he done time or something?"

"No, he hasn't done time," I said. "Crash is okay. A little bit corrupt, but okay."

The truth is that Crash had called right after I got home from Dr. Lewis's, and when he suggested I enter the "Dear Molly" contest, my eyebrows had gone up, too. I was, after all, a true crime writer, even if I hadn't written a true crime in years. But Crash was insistent. He convinced me that I had a chance.

"Look," Mungus said now. "You have more common sense than anybody I know. I'd take advice from you before I'd take it from Lee Iacocca. But this advice column thing . . . it's not you."

"Not me?"

"This is a thing women do," he said. "Writing advice in the newspaper."

"A man can do it," I said.

Just then something disgusting landed on Mungus's leg. A small child rushed over, grabbed it, tossed it to her pal, and ran off giggling.

"Okay," Mungus said, after he wiped his leg off with a napkin. "What I mean is . . ." Now he shifted his body and stared off as if he were about to tell me I had leukemia. He shoved three French fries into his mouth. "What I'm trying to say to you is that advice columnists are respectable people. Molly wasn't the smartest person in the world, and she wasn't the greatest writer, but she was a good person, and her audience sensed it."

"And I'm not?" I said.

Mungus put down his Big Mac and pushed his fries to one side. This was serious.

"Scotty," he said, "you're my friend and I adore you. If you were a woman, or even a very rich man, I'd marry you. But let's face it, you're a lot more like me than you are like Molly."

"Meaning?"

"Molly was a sweet, honest person. You and me, well, we're not garroting nurses in vacant lots at midnight, but let's face it, integrity is not our strong suit."

"Suit?" I said. "You're talking about the suit."

"No, I'm not."

"Yes, you are, you're talking about the suit." Years ago I bought a $398.00 suit at Jordan Marsh and the salesgirl had run it up as $3.98. I had never corrected her mistake, and Mungus had never let me forget it. He said that if I ever ran for president, it would come out.

"It's not just the suit," Mungus said. "It's the time we snuck into the Boston Garden. The way we always take two papers out of the newspaper box when we pay for one. All those little things."

"I could become more respectable," I said.

"Right," Mungus said. "Besides, you're not the contestant type. You've thrown away enough sweepstakes opportunities to fill Ed McMahon's swimming pool. I think you even tossed one that said 'Jeff Scutlandy, you are definitely a ten-million-dollar winner. This is not a trick.'"

"Okay, so I don't fall for every scam that comes in the mail the way you do," I said. "But this 'Dear Molly' thing is not like a sweepstakes where every loser with a pencil and an envelope has an equal chance. It's a talent search and the winner will be judged on merit, not plucked out of a mindless computer."

"It's still not you," Mungus said. "It's not worth the time it would take you to write the letter of application. The odds are incredible."

"The odds? You're the guy who picked Hocus Pocus to win the seventh race at Rockingham last Saturday, and you're worried about odds."

"Scotty, a zillion people will enter. You won't have a snowball's chance in a million."

"Bozos and bimbos!" I said. The woman with the cleavage looked up. I was talking too loud. "Most people," I said, lowering my voice, "cannot write a grocery list without making six grammatical errors."

"True," Mungus said, "but there will be a lot of writers, too."

"You think John Updike is going to enter this thing? Sure, there will be writers. But most of them are writing garden columns for the community shopper. I've published books, for God's sake."

"Yeah," Mungus said. "That's why you're so rich."

"Okay, so authors don't make much money," I said.

"Especially when they go four years without writing a book," Mungus chided.

"But syndicated columnists do. They need wheelbarrows just to go to the bank."

"Scotty, what is going on?"

"Going on? Nothing is going on. I'm just thinking about entering this contest, that's all."

"Yeah, well, you're real hyper about it. Why are you acting crazy? Is it these kids? Should I call the police and have them all thrown out?"

"I saw my doctor today," I said.

"Jesus. You're not going to tell me you have some terminal blood disease."

"He says I've got too much stress in my life."

"Stress?" Mungus said. The left eyebrow went up. "What the hell does a doctor know about stress? They all drive Porsches."

"He darkly implied that I should get a real job with a steady paycheck," I said.

"You mean the kind of thing where you actually have to get up in the morning and show up someplace?"

"Exactly."

"Are you going to do it?"

"Yes," I said. "That's why I'm so depressed."

Mungus bowed his head. "And that's why you've been thinking about this contest?"

"Yes."

"A desperate and futile last-ditch effort to avoid work?"

"Yes," I said again.

Of course, there had been other nights when I had skidded this close to captivity, only to veer away the next morning when I awoke renewed and again foolishly hopeful. But this time was different. Anne. Molly. My health. I was a middle-aged man who had spent his afternoon putting wooden blocks under his bed, and was spending his evening eating cheap hamburgers with the Legos crowd. This time was definitely different. I felt as if my spine had been snapped like a celery stick. Freelancing is a young man's game, Lewis had said, and I knew he was right.

Mungus looked up. "You're not going to start wearing a necktie, are you?"

"I might have to."

"God," Mungus said. "I'm sorry. I didn't realize things were that bad."

For a minute we ate in reverential silence. Mungus's appetite seemed to be undiminished by the shocking news, but clearly he was saddened. Mungus could certainly identify. From time to time he had taken his own fearful glances at the "Help Wanted" section. Now, witnessing my tragic situation was like seeing the soldier in front of him fall dead in the sand.

"If I ever have to get a job," he said, "I want it to be right here at McDonald's. All those housewives working the night shift. Can you imagine what must go on in the bun closet?" He crinkled the bushy eyebrows again so that they looked like caterpillars crawling across his forehead.

By the time we were done eating, most of the tots had been hauled home for baths. Mungus stood up. The wreckage of his Big Mac lay strewn across a napkin on the table.

"McCookies?" he said. "You know, to kind of wash away the sorrow of this job thing."

"Sure," I said.

Mungus was right, I thought as he walked off to get cookies. I wasn't fit to be an advice columnist. And I certainly had no chance of winning the job. There would be thousands of people applying for it, and maybe half of them wouldn't know their own ZIP code, but the other half would include a lot of clever and talented folk, and many of them would be good people like Molly. The whole idea of me entering was demented. Did I really need another rejection in my life? As a writer I had been weaned on rejection. As a husband I had been devastated by it. And as a friend I had been . . . well I didn't know what exactly, but Molly had given me the ultimate rejection, and I was in no mood for more.

In a moment Mungus was back. He stood by the table. The woman with the cleavage was leaning way over and Mungus wasn't even gaping at her, so I knew that something major was on his mind.

"Did you say that advice columnists make wheelbarrows full of money?" he asked.

"They do if they're nationally syndicated," I said.

He sat down and shoved a small box of cookies at me. Then he pulled a cookie out of his own little box. "Like how much money are we talking?"

"Molly was making a million a year," I said.

Now the eyebrows went as high as they could. "A million? Dollars? Every year?"

I explained about the syndication, the speaking engagements, the pamphlets, and the endorsements, as I had to Dr. Lewis.

"Molly had that kind of money?" Mungus said. "How come she didn't lend some to you?"

"She did," I said. "Long time ago. I never paid it back. She said forget it. I did. But I could never turn to her again for money."

"A million dollars," Mungus said. He reached into the pocket of his shirt and pulled out a snub-nosed pencil and a piece of paper. "Perhaps I was a bit hasty in my judgment," he said, jamming another cookie into his mouth. "Maybe you would be an ideal replacement for Molly. Now, how many people do you figure will enter this thing?"

"I don't know. Six thousand, I guess."

Whoever gets this job is going to be rich, I thought. And then: *Molly was rich. Did somebody kill her because she was rich?*

Now there was a kind of madness in Mungus's eyes and he leaned intensely over his paper, like a prisoner drawing an escape map. He wrote "6,000." "Okay," he said, "so let's say that six thousand people apply for the job. Would it be fair to say that three thousand of them will be unmitigated morons?"

"It depends on what you mean by morons," I said.

"You know, people who still send money to Jimmy Swaggart. That type."

"I guess," I said.

"And another two thousand will be well meaning, but hopeless," Mungus said. "High school English teachers who think they can write, drapery salesmen who think they've got their fingers on the pulse of the common man, defrocked clergymen, ex-hookers, lawyers. Okay, so that leaves a thousand."

"That's still a thousand to one," I said. Suddenly I was the doubter.

"Half the thousand will be therapists and Ph.D.s," Mungus said.

"So?"

"So? Did you ever read a textbook? Name me one Ph.D. in the Western Hemisphere who can write a simple declarative sentence in English."

"Good point," I said.

"So now there's five hundred contestants," Mungus went on, jotting his numbers on the crumpled paper, which I realized now was his overdue electric bill. The lady with the cleavage, and all the mothers and children, had left the restaurant, and now I could hear both the flat tip of Mungus's pencil scratching on the paper, and the sound of McCookies being crushed between his teeth. Suddenly he looked up, and his eyebrows were wiggling furiously.

"Does the *Patriot* want people to send a photo with their letter?"

"Yes," I said.

"Aha!" Mungus said, triumphantly. "Okay, so they want to see how you're going to look on the *Montel Williams Show* and the cover of *People* magazine."

"I suppose," I said, and now I was thinking: *there will be syndication money for the new Molly Collins, lecture money, money for showing up at supermarket openings.* Molly would understand my wanting to be rich, I told myself.

"So they'll throw out all the fatties and the uglies," Mungus said, "and maybe the nerdy types and the people with horrible acne scars all over their faces."

"Mungus," I said, "I appreciate the encouragement, but let's face it, there aren't that many repulsive-looking people in the world."

"There aren't? When was the last time you went into a Laundromat at night?"

"Okay," I said, "but no matter how you figure it, there would still be several hundred people in this thing besides me."

I had come into McDonald's thinking I had a chance, but now with Mungus telling me it was so, I was trying to talk myself out of the idea.

"I'm not done yet," Mungus said. He glanced around, as if the few remaining customers in McDonald's might try to steal his information.

"You know who else they'll throw out?" he said, speaking softly now, as if we were conspirators.

"Who?"

"The ones under thirty."

"Why?"

"Because people would say, 'He's not even thirty

years old, what the hell does he know about life?'
Nobody wants some snotty-nosed brat telling him which
girlfriend to dump. And they will also chuck everybody
who's over sixty because people would say, 'She's an old
lady, what does she know about today's problems?'
Nobody wants to take advice from a prune."

"What about Ann Landers and 'Dear Abby'?" I
countered. "They're both around seventy."

"They're entrenched," Mungus said. "It's like having
an old dog. It goes blind and deaf and you can't bring
yourself to shoot it. But when it dies you don't go to the
pet shop and buy a new one that's blind and deaf."

"Very sensitively put," I said.

"And don't forget," Mungus said, "Molly acquired
more readers in six years than those old gals did in thirty.
The country is mostly baby boomers and that's who they
want to hear from. They want to hear from you."

"Hmmm," I said. Mungus and I had switched sides,
but now I was starting to see it his way.

"So now we're down to a hundred people," Mungus
said. He stared at his paper. He chewed on his pencil. He
eyed my remaining cookies. "I figure seventy of them are
women."

"Why's that, Mungus?"

"Because most people think that giving advice is
woman's work," he said.

"Sounds familiar."

"But let's face it, the *Patriot* wants a man for this job.
They want something different. So you're not even
competing with all the women who enter. You going to
eat those cookies?"

When Mungus asks a question like that, he does not
wait for an answer. Now he reached across the table and
snapped up one of my cookies. "Let's go," he said.

It was a short drive back to the cottage. It was dark when we got home, and as we walked onto the raggedy porch, I felt watched. But I pushed the thought from my mind.

Mungus was still going on about the contest.

"So we're not really talking about six thousand people," he was saying as he pushed open the door and we walked into the living room. In the center of the room he pulled the string for the overhead, filling the room with light. "We're talking about thirty or forty guys. A dozen of them will be a little bit fruity, so they're out. You can write better than the rest. And you always look great on television."

"Mungus, I haven't been on television in three years," I said.

"And you're not tied down by another job," Mungus said. While he spoke he went to the downstairs closet and pulled out his indoor mini-golf set, and began placing the small plastic holes with little flags at odd places around the room. He handed me one of the plastic putters. "Plus, you know people at the *Patriot*. And finally, you are an experienced investigative reporter who has written about many true crimes." He smiled, prepared for his first putt, and said, "I rest my case."

"Investigative reporter? True crimes?" I said. "What the hell does any of that have to do with writing an advice column?"

"Come on, Scotty. I'm not stupid. Isn't that what this is all about? You want to win the contest so you can get inside the *Patriot* and snoop around about Molly's death."

Was that what this was all about? I wondered. These were strange times for me, and half the time I didn't know my own motives.

"What makes you think Molly's death was connected to her work?"

"I'm not saying it was," Mungus said. "I'm saying that you think it was. But let's face it, if Molly was murdered, and I'm not saying she was, it would have to be connected to work. Molly's personal life was about as exciting as cauliflower."

Mungus was about to make his first putt when we heard a popping sound and the living room window shattered. "Jesus Christ!" Mungus shouted. He lunged at me and practically picked me up as he threw me on the floor. He came down on top of me like a linebacker. "Somebody's shooting at us." Another shot came through the window.

"What the fuck?" he said.

"Molly," I said. "It's got something to do with Molly."

We lay flat on the floor. I had a mini-golf flag poking in my face. Mungus and I were so close that I couldn't tell which pounding was my heartbeat and which was Mungus's. Suddenly Mungus jumped up from the floor, leaped across the room, and grabbed for the string on the overhead light. Instead he got the lip of the glass globe around the light, and the whole works came ripping out of the ceiling. In the darkness I heard Mungus and the light fixture crash to the floor. "Can't shoot what you can't see," he said gleefully. Then he said, "Scotty, I don't normally approve of firearms, but maybe you'd better go get your gun."

In the darkness I worked my way up the stairs to my room and blindly fished around in my closet until I found the Smith & Wesson. By the time I came back down with the gun, my eyes were adjusting to the weak light provided by the moon. I tried to imagine the shooter outside our window. Lillian Gilmartin with a gun?

Dracut? Crash Galovitch? None of this made any sense. I couldn't visualize any of them crouching out there with a gun. All I could see was the Reverend Fred McHale, and in my imagination he didn't even have a gun, just that damned knife.

Mungus crawled over to the front door, and I joined him there. We sat facing the door, with just enough room for someone to open it. I held the gun in two hands, cradled between my knees. If he or she came through the door, I'd shoot without waiting. Or would I? I wondered. I'm the guy who takes hornets to the front door and shoos them out of the house instead of killing them, and I'm going to mercilessly fire thirty-eight-caliber bullets into some human in the dark? Right, Scotty. "Let's go get him," Mungus said.

"Huh?"

"He's still there. We didn't hear any car pull out."

"He'll shoot us."

"Yeah, you're probably right," Mungus said. "But if we don't go get him, we'll never know who he is or when he's watching us."

"I don't want to go out there," I said to Mungus.

We sat there for two hours before we were convinced that the gunman was gone.

CHAPTER 8

For two days after the shooting I couldn't stop twitching. I stayed away from windows. I kept my pistol handy. I even rehearsed for the gunman's next visit, by placing the revolver on my desk and then grabbing it to see how long it took to get it into firing position. I rearranged the furniture in my office. I poured my paper clips from a box to a bowl. I dusted every surface, and I put the books on my shelves in alphabetical order, by author. I did everything I could to perpetuate the illusion that I had control of the world around me.

Mungus, in the meantime, seemed cautious, but less troubled, by the event. He put an old wooden duck pin next to his bed, to pummel intruders, but he never took it with him, the way I probably would have. We took cold comfort from the police report, which said that the angle of the shots showed that the shooter was aiming for the ceiling, as if he were trying to scare us, not kill us.

When I calmed down I decided that I needed to try harder to find out what the hell was going on. So I called Crash Galovitch and asked him to meet me for lunch. It wasn't that I suspected Crash of anything wicked, or even that I thought he had lied when he said he was sure that Molly wasn't murdered. But I knew that if sinister webs were being spun at the *Patriot*, chances were that Crash could name the spiders.

"I don't want to be seen in Boston with you," Crash said on the phone. "It wouldn't look good."

"Wouldn't look good?"

"You're entering the 'Dear Molly' contest, right?"

"Wrong," I said.

"What do you mean, wrong? You've got a great chance. Don't be a schmuck."

"Well, I might enter it," I said. "I was talking it over with Mungus, but I was interrupted when someone started shooting at us."

"Shooting? What the hell you talking about, shooting?"

"I'll explain when I see you," I said. Since Crash was talking to me from his office at the *Patriot*, it didn't seem like a good time to discuss it.

"Okay, but we can't meet in Boston," Crash said. "It wouldn't look right."

"Wouldn't look right?"

"You in the contest, and me, I'm the publicity guy for the whole thing. Wouldn't look right."

He suggested that on Friday night we meet at Rockingham racetrack, which is where Crash spent most of his Friday nights, anyhow.

During the half-hour drive from Plum Island to Rockingham, in Salem, New Hampshire, I thought a lot about Joe "Crash" Galovitch. Crash was a hard guy to figure. We had been buddies for a while in Florida. We had played a lot of golf at a little course on Alton Road, for ten bucks a hole. We had played poker with his friends. But I'd always felt that either I never got to know Crash real well, or that he was as shallow as a saucer, one of those people about whom there is little to be learned. Crash was a practical joker, and the most revealing moment I could recall with him was when we were driving up to Lauderdale one day and he told me that some of his jokes had really hurt people and that it didn't bother him. "But," he had added, "it bothers me a lot that it doesn't bother me."

We had only known each other a short time when Crash realized that my low-paying magazine and news-paper connections and his high-paying unconnected clients could create synergy for us, if we were willing to overlook a few ethical considerations, which we were. That's when I began writing articles about Crash's clients and he began kicking back fees to me. As a result we spent a lot of time on the phone, and that's how he got his name.

Crash liked to tell people that he got his name from being a race-car driver, but that was fiction. The truth is that I gave him the name because of the way he hung up a phone. He'd have a perfectly civilized conversation with you, but when it was over he would slam down the phone as if it had suddenly caught fire. I called it crashing the phone and I named him Crash Galovitch.

After we drifted apart, Crash fell into some serious debt. He divorced his wife, sold his sailboat and his agency, and took a job as public relations director for a pack of millionaire doctors in Sylvania, Ohio. From there he went to the job at the *Boston Patriot*.

The more I thought about Crash on the drive to Rockingham, the more I realized I was searching his past for some hint of murderous intent in his present. I also realized that there were many people in my life whom I didn't know a lot about.

You can't phone out from the track, so a mile before I got there I pulled into the parking lot of a Li'l Peach store and called Joan from a pay phone. It had been a few days since we had been able to sneak some time together, and I missed her. When Joan answered I asked, "Is Mrs. Espresso there?" which was code.

"I'm afraid you've got the wrong number," Joan said, which meant, "I can't talk, my husband is home."

I hung up, but at least I had heard her voice, and Joan knew I was thinking of her.

When I got to the huge parking lot at Rockingham, it was jammed, but I pulled into the preferred parking area and paid the buck fifty so I could be near the entrance. A small privilege, but it made me feel as if I were not a pauper. I took the escalator up to the clubhouse, walked past a dozen guys in wheelchairs, and stood at the top of the entrance to the seating area, looking down at descending rows of tables and chairs. I saw Crash waving to me from a small table in the first row, next to the glass and right over the finish line. The tote board flashed ten minutes to post time.

Crash had always been a thin and hungry-looking man, the kind that women like to mother. As I walked down to meet him, I could see that he had lost a lot of hair since I'd last seen him, and his smooth, dark skin was finally starting to show some age, but he still had those excited, darting eyes that the ladies liked.

The first thing Crash said to me was "Verbatim in the eighth. That's my pick of the day. A guaranteed winner. Guaranfuckingteed."

We shook hands. "Shitfuck," he said, "it's good to see you."

I sat down and Crash dealt out a few snapshots of his kids, now grown up. Then he signaled a waitress. He ordered wine, and I, with the ghost of Dr. Lewis hovering over me, ordered decaffeinated coffee.

"Decaf?" Crash said with a sneer. "That's like going to a whorehouse and not getting laid."

I had a few questions to ask Crash, but before I could ask them, he dived into his handicapping with a fervor that was frightening. The Racing Form was spread across the table like a map in a war room, and on top of that Crash had his own homemade charts, with all kinds of colored lines and meaningful numbers on them.

"See," he said, "I've got this system. Most people make their bets entirely on logical things like past performances, bandages, blinkers, and so forth, right? Other people, mostly women, they bet hunches, the jockey's name, the color of the blanket, that kind of shit. But they're both wrong, see, because they're only using one side of their brain. I use both sides. Plus the rump test."

"The rump test?"

"Sure," Crash said. "I look for a good, high, strong rump that kind of bounces when the horse is parading. If one horse has an outstanding rump, I go with that."

Then Crash ignored me for several minutes while he studied the Racing Form. Does he even know that I didn't come to bet on horses?" I wondered.

"Recycled Trash," Crash said finally. "What the hell kind of a name is that for a horse?" He looked up from the form, the wild eyes glancing around to see if somebody knew something he didn't. "What's this, a six-thousand-dollar race? The horse has been running at ten and twelve thousand, and he's got a pretty decent rump. Hmmm."

The waitress returned, and Crash sipped white wine out of a plastic glass, while I smugly drank my decaf. I had accepted the fact that Crash would be unapproachable until after the first race. I picked a horse called Joan's Luck, and when Crash went to the betting window, I gave him my two bucks.

Recycled Trash and Joan's Luck finished out of the money. Crash looked shaken. He tossed his ticket to the floor as if it had been bought with the last five-dollar bill he would ever see. He sipped more wine. Then the smile came back to his face. "Next race," he said optimistically. "Next race."

After he had done his calculating and decided on a horse called Familiar Quotes in the second race, Crash could relax. He pushed his papers aside, lit up a small plastic-tipped cigar, and said, "So, tell me about this shooting."

"Mungus and I were in the cottage, talking about me maybe entering the contest."

"Good," Crash said. "Do it."

"And some psycho started shooting through the window. We got low real fast. Mungus hit the floor so hard he got a bloody nose. Police came over and found the bullets in the ceiling. The psycho was using a hunting rifle."

"The ceiling?"

"Yeah. They figure he crouched down outside the cottage and shot up through the top of the window."

"Why?"

"Either he was the world's worst shot or he wanted to

make damn sure he didn't kill anybody. They think he was just trying to scare us."

"And you figure it had something to do with the Molly thing."

"What do you think?"

"Maybe it's someone you wrote about years ago. You said nasty things about a lot of felons when you were writing true crimes."

"Another Fred McHale? Not likely," I said. "It's connected to Molly."

It wasn't until after Familiar Quotes finished second by a head, and Crash damn near fainted, that I got down to my business. I bought him another glass of wine and asked, "Did Molly know that Lawrence Dracut was buying the *Patriot*?"

"Why?" Crash said. He glanced hatefully at the table next to us, where three guys were practically dancing because they had won a two-dollar trifecta that paid eight hundred and fifty bucks.

"I figure she must have," I said. "The way I see it, she found out that Dracut was taking over. Molly was too classy to work for a maggot like Dracut, so she decided to quit the *Patriot*. I think she was going to announce it at a party she had scheduled before she died."

"I don't know about that," Crash said. "But yes, she would have known that Dracut was taking over."

"Why?"

"Because the three syndicated columnists, especially Molly, were one of the paper's biggest assets."

"And?"

"Anybody who wanted to buy the *Patriot* would try to sign them to a long-term contract before deciding what the paper was worth. Molly was working on a handshake, and if she didn't agree to a long-term deal, that would make the paper less valuable."

"So my theory makes sense," I said.

"Not if your theory includes murder," Crash said. "See, Scotty, you couldn't make Molly come back to the *Patriot* by murdering her. She's still gone. Whether Molly was quitting or not, there certainly was no benefit to the paper in her dying."

"That's not quite true," I said. "The contest."

Suddenly Crash got nervous. "Look, Scotty, don't fuck around with the contest, okay. The contest is great. It's got nothing to do with any of this."

"Whose idea was it?"

"Dracut's," Crash said. And then, "Okay, so the guy is a hustler, granted. But the contest is a good idea. It's worth a fortune in publicity, and it will make it easy for us to sell Molly's replacement to the syndicate papers."

"I wonder how easy it would be to sell her replacement if the real Molly Collins were still alive and writing her column for another paper," I said.

Crash had no answer.

"Jesus, I don't know," he said. He put his hands to his temple. "All I know is Molly is going to be just as dead whether you are right or wrong. I want this contest to go smoothly. And you should, too. Have you thought about what it would mean to you if you won it?"

"I've thought about it," I admitted. "All that money, the fame. It makes me feel guilty just thinking about it."

After the third race I ordered fried chicken. Screw Dr. Lewis, I thought. Crash kept on betting. It was the same bet every time. "Five dollars to win," he would announce, before marching off to line up at the betting windows with his program clutched in one hand and my pathetic two-dollar bet in the other. While hundreds of screaming horse fans watched the races, I watched Crash, and each time his horse fell off the pace, a look of genuine terror came into his face, as if he personally would be whipped for the horse's failure to win. In the sixth race Crash won when a nine-to-one pick, Martin's Elf, came flying out of the backstretch to close it by a length. Crash was ecstatic, and like a true gambler, he was convinced that this was the beginning of a major winning streak. After he placed his bet for the seventh, he was able to tear himself away from his charts and forms once more and return to planet Earth.

Another cigar was lighted. Another glass of wine was poured. We kidded each other about the old days of puff pieces and kickbacks.

"I never felt guilty about any of that shit," Crash said. "How about you?"

"I did for a while," I said. "But I got over it."

Crash lost the seventh, eighth, ninth, tenth, and eleventh race, and with each race he grew more furious with the losing horse. By the time Banana Pudding was pulling up the rear in the eleventh, Crash was screaming such obscene vitriol at the poor pathetic beast that even I was shocked. It was hard to believe that a guy could get that hot over a bunch of five-dollar bets. I stooped down and picked up one of his losing tickets. The bet was for a hundred dollars. I picked up another. A hundred bucks. I picked up more. They were all for a hundred bucks.

"Jesus, Crash," I said. "What the hell are you doing, betting that kind of money?"

For a long time he didn't speak, he just dabbed at his sweaty face with a napkin that had a cartoon of a horse on it. Then he threw some wine into his mouth. Finally, when he was composed, he said, "Look, Scotty, you've dealt with a lot of criminals, right? Is it true about loan sharks? Do they really break guys' legs, or is that just in the movies?"

"How much are you into them for?"

"Eighty thousand," he said. "Most of it I left on the tables at Bally's in Atlantic City. Some of it's here. Fucking state's got its share, too."

"The state?"

"Lottery tickets," he explained. "So is it true, do they really mutilate people?"

"Sometimes," I said.

"Jesus," he said.

Crash was tapped out, so we skipped the last race. We walked out slowly, squeezed into a wedge of other losers who also had no money for the twelfth race. Then we stood out in the chilly parking lot, mostly lying to each other about women we had slept with since our last meeting. Then he told me about a woman he'd slept with a year ago, and I think that was true because he got sad when he said her name. I told him I was seeing someone, but I didn't tell him the name. Soon his optimism returned.

"Look, pal, don't worry about me," he said. "The money, I mean. I know a shark in Jacksonville. I can get the money from him to pay off the local shark. That will buy me a couple of months. Then I got something down the road that's going to pay off big."

I smiled. Gamblers, I thought. They've always got something down the road that's going to pay off big.

We shook hands. "Sorry about the hysterics," he said. "Half the nags I bet on will be Alpo by this time next week." And then, "Good luck with the contest."

"Thanks," I said as we started to move apart. "But me as a nationally syndicated advice columnist? It's the ultimate long shot."

I watched Crash pull out of the parking lot. He had a 1988 blue Toyota Corolla. I wrote down the plate number.

CHAPTER 9

"The ultimate long shot?" Mungus said a few nights later. "How can you say that? You're perfect for the job."

We were in the living room and Mungus had just built a fire in the fieldstone fireplace. He wiped off his can of beer with one hand, and my arm with the other, then started tugging me toward my small office behind the living room. "Come on, you said it yourself, you're a writer, you helped Molly with letters. People always turn to you for advice."

It was the night before the deadline for applying for the Molly job, and Mungus desperately wanted me to write a letter of application. When we got into my office, he quickly pulled down the shade, forced me into the swivel chair at my desk, and then flopped like a dolphin onto my couch.

"Write the letter, Scotty," he said. He held the can of Coors in his hand.

"Why?"

"Look," he said, "you're my friend and I'm biased, okay. But I really do believe that you've got a lot of good qualities that you've been hiding lately. You could be a success at this thing, whether it helps you find Molly's murderer or not."

It was the first time that Mungus had acknowledged that Molly was murdered. I guess a couple of rifle shots through the window can be a rapid conversion experience for anyone.

As I sat there staring first at my computer and then at Mungus, the smell of the fire came into the cozy office, and, despite everything, the cottage felt safe and comforting. In the days since my visit with Crash, I'd been able to put more and more distance between me and my gun. Now it was hidden under a musty cushion on a rummage-sale chair in the living room.

"Remember when I first discovered that I was getting a pot belly?" Mungus said.

"You were hysterical."

"And I tried everything."

I remembered. For weeks Mungus had carried on like a schoolgirl. He tried weights. He tried swimming. He tried fat-reduction suits and anticellulite pills and even some capsules he got by mail that claimed to remove fat in the middle of the night while the fat person was sleeping. But beer, pizza, and Kentucky Fried Chicken, extra crispy, were too much to overcome.

"And I came to you, ready to stick my neck in a noose over the whole thing," Mungus said. "And do you remember what you told me? You said all I had to do was love myself and everything else would take care of itself. You said if I showed my love by treating myself to pork chops and onion rings, that was okay. And if I showed my love by keeping in shape, that was okay, too. If I just loved myself, things would be the way they were supposed to be."

"I said that? It sounds more like Molly."

"You and Molly weren't that different," Mungus said. "It was you."

"I suppose it was," I said. It was a me I could barely remember.

"That was the best advice anybody ever gave me," Mungus said. "It made me realize that the pot belly wasn't the problem. The problem was the way I felt about it. You ought to enter this Molly thing. You'd be great at it."

It had been a long time since I'd been great at anything, I thought. Above my desk was a reminder. It was my poster-sized blowup of the most scathing review I'd gotten for the Fred McHale book. The reviewer had exhausted every clever insult in his book and had finished with "Scotland did not come close to giving this story the Norman Mailer or Shana Alexander treatment it deserves," and beneath those words, in red Magic Marker, I had violently scrawled the words "Scotland also did not get a half-million-dollar advance to write the story, you moron."

"Look," I said to Mungus, "are you just blowing smoke up my ass, or do you really think I'd make a good 'Dear Molly'?"

Mungus smiled. "Write the application letter. The worst that can happen is you lose thirty-two cents in postage." There was a moment of silence, and then Mungus rose dramatically from the couch. He stood somewhat unsteadily beside me and looked down into my eyes. "Three seconds left," he said. "Boston Garden. Seventh game of the NBA championship playoffs. The Lakers have a one-point lead. You have the ball. What are you going to do, Scotty, let the fans down? You going to let the boys from L.A. have the crown?" When it came to the Celtics, both Mungus and I were living in a glorious past.

But I had no choice. I booted up my computer and wrote the letter to Lawrence Dracut.

I began with my writing background, the books, the personal columns, etc. Then I gave him my view on advice columns.

"Of course, writing skills are no substitute for compassion, wisdom, and knowledge," I wrote. "You need someone who is responsible in the advice he will give, yet aware that his columns exist to entertain as well as inform. You need someone who can be witty without being biting, and wise without being pompous. You need someone who is well informed, but not too proud to call on experts when he needs help. I am all of these things."

I have never been comfortable with immodesty, but when you apply for a job, it's either brag or be shown to the door.

Then I wrote a paragraph about how honesty was the most important quality an advice columnist could have, and how I certainly had that. I wound up with my age, marital status, and the fact that I had no children.

All the while Mungus stood behind me like a shift supervisor, peering over my shoulder as the little white letters appeared on the blue screen of my computer.

"So what do you think?" I asked when the letter was drafted.

He took a swig from his can of Coors.

"The truth?" he asked.

"Yeah, yeah, the truth," I said impatiently.

He handed me the can. I sucked some beer out of it, thinking surely Dr. Lewis didn't mean this when he said "no alcohol."

"The letter is a P.O.S.," Mungus said.

"P.O.S.?"

"Piece of shit," he explained.

"Thanks," I said.

"Okay, let me amend that," Mungus said. "It's not a total piece of shit. But it is duller than sex with Marilyn Quayle. There's some good things in it, but if I were the *Patriot*, I wouldn't hire you."

"Why?"

"Because it's just you saying you can do the job. There's no proof. Show, don't tell."

"Writing tips?" I snapped. "I ask you for help and you give me rules of style. I'm not just telling them. I'm going to include copies of some of that sensitive-man stuff I wrote a few years ago when I was Mr. Feminist."

"Good idea," Mungus said. "But it's not enough. You didn't even tell them you were a friend of Molly's."

"No," I said. "I'm not going to cash in on Molly. They know we were friends. That's enough."

"Okay," Mungus said. "But the letter isn't you. It sounds like an application for a job."

"Mungus, it *is* an application for a job. If I put the real me on paper, do you think they'd hire me?"

"You've got a point," Mungus said. "Still. It needs something." He grabbed the can of beer and flopped down onto my office couch once more. He wiggled until he was comfortable, and then he gently put the beer can to his lips as if it were a warm breast. He stared at the bare wood ceiling as if something were written there. Then he flashed a moronic smile at me.

"Scotty," he said, "I know you can do this job because I've heard you give people advice. But the *Boston Patriot* doesn't know that. They think you're just some failure from Plum Island who's looking to make an easy buck."

"Well, what can I do?" I said. "I can't just make up counseling credits."

Mungus closed his eyes and for a few peaceful seconds kissed the rim of his beer can. I thought I had lost him. "Now that," he said, opening his eyes and pointing the beer can at me, "is a very good idea."

"Just make up credentials?" I said. "That's lying."

Mungus stared at me. His eyes were getting real wet-looking now. "Have you seen the paper today?" he said.

"What about it?"

"Six terrified tourists were sucked into the sky by a UFO in Memphis. A baboon girl married a wolf boy. And in Oklahoma there's a pickup truck with the power to heal people."

He smiled again, closed his eyes briefly, and nodded his head, as if to say, "So there!"

"Is there a point?" I asked.

"The point is that newspapers lie all the time, so why shouldn't you lie to them?"

"You're talking about some rag at the Food World checkout counter."

"It's a newspaper, isn't it? Have you seen the *Patriot* since Dracut took over? They're all liars. It's just a matter of degree."

"So you're saying I should lie to them because they lie to me."

"Absolutely," Mungus said. "It's either that or put on a tie and go to work for a living and let Molly's murderer roam the streets to kill again."

"What you're talking about is deceit."

"Hey, don't knock deceit. It worked fine for five of our last six presidents."

"Maybe you've got a point," I said.

"Of course I've got a point." He sat up now, all excited. "Look, I'm not saying that lying is always good. I'm just saying that this is one of those times when lying makes a lot of sense. You have certain counseling abilities, but there are small-minded people out there who aren't interested in ability. They're interested in pieces of paper that say you were exposed to the information that could give you ability. College degrees, that sort of thing. You're never going to convince them that they are imbeciles. So it makes sense to lie. It won't change your qualifications and you'll still have to survive on your own merit."

Now Mungus was really worked up. It seemed as if he was a lot more interested in me being the new Molly Collins than I was.

"If I beat the six-thousand-to-one odds," I said.

"You'll beat them. Besides, if you don't get the job, then the lies won't matter one way or the other."

Mungus was right. The lying wouldn't really change anything. It would just give me the fair shot that I had a right to. Without counseling credits of some sort I wouldn't have a chance of becoming the next Molly Collins.

I turned to face the screen on my computer again. For a moment it looked like the accusing face of God. I stretched my arm toward Mungus, and he put the can of beer in my hand. I swallowed the last of the beer. Mungus grabbed the empty can, shrieked "Larry Bird!" and slam-dunked it into my wastebasket. Then he went to the kitchen for more.

When he came back he dropped three wine coolers on my desk and carried a six-pack of beer to the couch with him. Mungus made himself comfortable.

I inserted a new paragraph in my letter and read the words to Mungus as I tapped them out on the keyboard.

"I spent three years as a counselor in private practice," I said.

"Tell them you're a psychiatrist," Mungus said.

"I can't tell them that."

"Okay. But counselor doesn't sound very impressive. It sounds like you teach kids to make ceramic candy dishes at camp."

"You're right," I said. I reached under my desk and hauled out the Boston Yellow Pages. I opened the phone book to "Counselors." "How's this," I said, reading phrases from an ad. "I spent three years as an Independent Licensed Clinical Social Worker."

"Sounds good," Mungus said. "What the hell does it mean?"

"I don't know."

"Tell them it was in Albuquerque, New Mexico," Mungus said.

I added Albuquerque, New Mexico, and read the sentence back to Mungus.

"Still needs something," he said. Then he shouted. "Kevin McHale!" and shot an empty beer can at my wastebasket. It went in. "Swish!" he announced gleefully.

I glanced at the Yellow Pages again. One counselor noted in his ad that he had specialized in personal and family counseling. Another boasted that she was a member of the American Association for Marriage and Family Therapy. I took a swallow of wine cooler and finished my paragraph.

"How's this?" I said. "For three years I worked as a Licensed Independent Clinical Social Worker in private practice in Albuquerque, New Mexico. I specialized in personal and family counseling. I am a member of the American Association for Marriage and Family Therapy."

"Impressive," Mungus said. "Put in that you graduated from Vanderbilt University."

"Why?"

"I had a girlfriend named Roz once who graduated from Vanderbilt. So we know that it is a place that a person can graduate from."

I added Vanderbilt University to my history.

I read the entire letter back to Mungus, and we agreed that even though it was now full of lies, it was still dull.

"But that's okay," Mungus said. "Later you can show them how clever you are. For now you've got to convince them that you're not the type that will advise fifteen-year-old girls to have sex with middle-aged writers." Then his eyes just about doubled in size. "God," he said. "If you become 'Dear Molly' and you come across as real sensitive and understanding, you'll be getting letters from women all over the country who want to have your baby. What an incredible job."

I printed the letter.

After I made a copy and addressed the envelope, I handed it to Mungus so he could kiss it for good luck. Mungus finished off another beer, then he screamed "Robert Parrish!" and he took a hook shot with an empty beer can and that went in.

After that we put a Kenny G album into the new CD player that Mungus had just bought on credit at Sears. I sat on the floor with my back against the couch so I'd be more comfortable, and also below the line of fire if bullets came through the window again. Mungus stayed on the couch. We talked and drank and slowly descended into drunkenness. We had our standard discussion about how there could possibly be a universe. "I mean, where did it come from?" Mungus kept saying. "And where was it the day before it got here?"

Later, on a more mundane level, Mungus said, "There's just one thing I want out of this Molly thing."

"What's that?" I said. I knew it didn't matter. Even before I sealed the envelope, I knew what a futile business this was. The dullness of the letter, the thousands of applicants, and the downward direction of my life, all indicated that I was wasting my time. Suddenly the letter, the investigation, everything, seemed pointless.

"If you become 'Dear Molly,' or 'Dear Scotty,' and you're a celebrity, will you hire me as one of those guys who hang around and go out for coffee now and then? You know, a real parasite, like those guys Elvis had around, a sort of combination bodyguard and stooge."

"Sure," I said, feeling bad for Mungus, because he actually believed I had a chance of winning.

CHAPTER 10

"Scotty, what the hell is it?" Hattie Slater asked when she finally answered her phone at *Glitz* magazine. As usual Hattie sounded as if she had been dragged out of a hot shower to come to the phone.

"I've got a great story idea," I said.

"So? Write me a query letter like every other freelancer," she said. Hattie had a way of saying freelancer that made it sound like *maggot*.

Though Hattie and I were, in our own queer way, friends, that had never stopped her from putting the screws to me whenever that was what would work best for her. Though Hattie was convinced that freelance writers ranked just below the slugworm on the evolutionary scale, as a magazine editor, she understood that using freelance writers made good economic sense, much as slavery had in the last century.

"I will put it in a letter," I said, "but I just wanted to screen the idea first."

"Screen it, bullshit," Hattie said. "You want to beat everybody else. What is it?" Then, "Hold on a second, I've got a real phone call on the other line."

This is Hattie, I thought as I listened to elevator music over the phone. She was a cantankerous little bitch, an ex-newspaper editor who made Lou Grant look like a fairy princess. Hattie was a dwarfish woman, with an eagle's nest of rust-colored hair and a brain as big as a Buick. She liked to work ninety-seven hours a day and had little patience for those who worked less.

However, I knew I couldn't be too self-righteous, because I was calling her for my own devious reasons. My real goal was to get an assignment that would allow me to interview Lawrence Dracut, just as I had interviewed Lillian Gilmartin. I wanted to find out if Dracut was capable of murder, and whether or not he owned a rifle. Crash Galovitch had told me that the contest was Dracut's idea. I knew it must have occurred to Dracut that a Molly Collins replacement would bring a lot more cash to the *Patriot* if the replacement didn't have to compete with the original. So this call to Hattie was, I told myself, part of my noble investigation into my friend's murder.

But, less nobly, I also wanted to become a regular writer for *Glitz*, where I had already published two stories. The bills were piling up and I needed assignments to hold me over until the dreaded day of full-time employment. I was, at least, rational enough to know I had no real shot at the Molly job, though I did fantasize about it.

"Now, what's this great idea?" Hattie said when she came back on the line.

"Molly Collins," I said.

"She's dead," Hattie said, as if that should end the conversation.

"I know she's dead, Hattie. For Christ's sake, she was

a friend of mine. But the *Boston Patriot* is running a nationwide contest to find a replacement."

"So?"

"What do you mean, so? This is a great *Glitz* story. Cabdrivers and hairdressers all think they are so good at giving advice. Thousands of them will enter. It's the great American dream. All of a sudden some nobody will be plucked from obscurity, become a household name with national syndication, appearances on the Merv Griffin show. Every hairstylist and cabdriver in the country thinks he or she can be an advice columnist, and they're going to be very interested in seeing who gets their dream job."

"Merv Griffin hasn't been on for twenty years," Hattie said. "What the hell planet are you living on?"

"Okay, okay, 'Live with Regis and Kathy Lee,' whatever. The point is that if you put this story on the cover, you'll blow *People* magazine out of the water. I could interview some of the people who applied for the job, find out why they think they're qualified to be the next 'Dear Molly.' Then I could interview people at the *Patriot*, like Lawrence Dracut. Then we could follow it up. I could write another story when they are down to their finalists. Build up the suspense. Maybe conduct a reader poll: 'Who do you think should be the next Molly Collins?' that sort of thing. Ask Madonna and Willard Scott who they would vote for. Joe Galovitch, the PR guy at the *Patriot*, is a friend of mine. I'm sure he'll give me all the inside stuff."

"No shit, Scotty?" Hattie said. "You mean you can actually get a PR flak to talk to you about the very thing he's trying to publicize?"

"Okay, never mind about that. But what about the article? What do you think?"

"It's in the bag," Hattie said.

"Huh?"

"It's in the bag."

"What bag? What the hell are you talking about?"

"The bag, for Christ's sake. The contest is fixed."

"How do you know?"

"Instinct," Hattie said. "These things are always fixed. They already know who they want."

"You're just cynical," I said. I felt guilty. Here I was the pot calling the kettle cynical. "Of course it's not fixed. They wouldn't dare."

"Scotty," Hattie said, speaking slowly now, as if English were my second language. "How many people do you think used to read Molly Collins every day?"

"I don't know. Fifty million?"

"Try ninety-five million," Hattie said. "She got more letters than Congress and Rush Limbaugh combined. She was in twelve hundred newspapers. She was in places like Uganda and Reykjavik, for God's sake. She peddled more pamphlets than the Jehovah's Witnesses, and she had to split the money with the *Patriot*."

"So what's the point?" I said.

"The point is that Molly was making buckets of money for the *Patriot*, and if they're careful, they'll replace her with another goose who will lay more golden eggs. Do you think they are going to put that kind of power into the hands of someone they don't know, someone who can turn around in a year and say, 'Thanks, fellows, for making me the new Molly Collins, I think I'll just syndicate myself from here on in, have a nice day?' Of course not. They'll run a contest, milk it for the publicity, and then announce that some bimbo from Decatur is the new Molly Collins. Whoever she is, you can bet that she's performing oral sex on the publisher or teaching aerobics to his wife. Or the other way around. They are going to own her ass, I can guarantee it."

"You've got it all wrong," I said. "The thing isn't fixed. I think they are going to do something daring, like replace Molly with a man."

Hattie sighed. "Jesus, Scotty, what time this morning did they drop you off the turnip truck? Have you ever heard of Ann Landers?" she said.

"What about her?"

"And no doubt you've heard of 'Dear Abby'?"

"Yeah, yeah, sure. So?"

"How about Dr. Ruth? Joyce Brothers? Beth Whitehead?"

"How about getting to a point?" I said.

"Scotty, look real closely there. There's a pattern. They all sit down to pee. This kind of thing works best with a woman, it always has. Now, how many companies do you know that say, 'Hey guys, let's not go with the thing that's always made tons of money, let's try something different?' "

"Different is what gets publicity," I argued. "If they choose a man, it will be the publicity coup of the decade."

"They'll get publicity out of the contest no matter what they do," Hattie screeched. "Publicity is what the contest is all about, so they can convince their syndicate newspapers that there is still a demand for this product. Otherwise, they would just hire their bimbo and put her to work."

"Okay," I said, "let's say the contest is fixed. So what? Let's do the story anyhow."

There was a long pause.

"Scotty," Hattie said, "You've been staring at your VDT too long. Either that, or you've got your brain up your ass today. If this thing is a fraud, and we do a big story, and they get caught, *Glitz* will be the laughingstock of the industry."

"Then you're saying you don't want the story?"

"No, I'm not saying that. I'm saying shove the story up your ass."

"Hattie, I could use the money," I said.

"Excuse me," Hattie said, "but you must have mistaken me for someone who gives a shit."

"I see," I said, and we both hung up.

I immediately picked up the phone and called Crash Galovitch. "Crash," I said, "I just talked to my friend Hattie Slater at *Glitz*. I've got an assignment to write a piece about the contest. Can you set me up with an interview with Lawrence Dracut?"

Crash was thrilled about the publicity. I figured I could always tell him later that the story had been killed. I needed to see Dracut. Later that day Crash called and told me he would set something up as soon as Dracut got back from some business in Minneapolis.

On the following Friday I learned that there had not been six thousand applicants for Molly's job. There had been eighteen thousand, five hundred and twelve. I learned this when I was sitting in a king-sized bed with Joan Bentley, reading *USA Today* at the Honeysuckle Motel in Milford, a AAA-approved little forty-room affair that had prints of Rocky Mountain vistas on all the bedroom walls. Joan and I had come for coffee, bagels, and sex. This had become a Friday morning ritual with us. Find a delicatessen. Check into a motel. Sit in bed, eat bagels, read the newspaper, make love. Fridays were ideal because on Fridays Joan's husband always drove to Norwich, Connecticut, to visit his mother who had been dying of cancer for two decades.

"Eighteen thousand, five hundred and twelve," I said to Joan, staring ruefully at the story about the contest.

"What?" Joan said. She had her *New York Times* spread out on the bed, overlapping my *USA Today*.

"More than eighteen thousand people applied for Molly's job. It's here in the paper."

"I know," she said. "Isn't it incredible? They've got huge boxes of mail lined up against the wall in Molly's old office."

"I'm one of them," I said.

"One of what?"

"The eighteen thousand, five hundred and twelve."

"You entered?" Joan said. "You're kidding."

"No."

"Why didn't you tell me?"

"I don't know," I said. "Fear of failure, I guess."

"Well, I think it's great," she said. She thought it over. "My niece entered, too."

"The one who's trying to get her life together?"

"Yes. She's twenty."

"Great. She'll probably win."

"I think they should pick you," Joan said. "You'd be great. You always give me good advice."

I still hadn't gotten used to the idea that this woman I was falling for adored me at a time when I felt like a twelve-karat dud.

"Do you think you have a chance?" Joan asked.

"No," I said.

Eighteen thousand, five hundred and twelve, I thought as I read the story. And that number only included the people who had beaten the deadline. The hopes of several thousand more dreamers lay dead in unopened mailbags. Eighteen thousand, I thought. I'd be lucky if they even found my letter, never mind read it.

Apparently, my clever idea . . . lying . . . was one of the least novel approaches to the "Dear Molly" job. Dracut told *USA Today* that many would-be advice givers had sent cakes, cookies, and various highly caloric bribes along with their letters. A deranged woman from Nebraska had shown up in person, naked, with an original and two photocopies of her letter strategically posted on her body. Quintuplets in Maine had proposed that the five of them replace Molly. "Five heads," they wrote, "are better than one." The well-known wife of a United States senator had also applied for the job, darkly implying that political screws could be tightened if the *Boston Patriot* didn't do the right thing. And, my favorite, a couple from Colorado had threatened to commit a double suicide by swallowing lye if they didn't get the job. I read on, thinking I would come to something like "and a pathetically transparent washed-up Massachusetts writer lied about his credentials, claiming to have been a counselor in New Mexico." But even that much notoriety was kept from me. And by the time I finished reading the story aloud to Joan, I had accepted the fact that any chance I'd had of becoming a rich and famous advice columnist, and the heroic solver of the famous Molly Collins murder, had been canceled like a postage stamp. I had never rated my chances high, but this was a chilling reminder that I had to look for a job.

"I suppose they will give the job to a professional therapist," Joan said after I read her the story.

"Probably," I said. It did not seem necessary to tell Joan about my phony credentials. The fact that I was an unrepentant liar might make her think less of me.

"Can you think of any reason why someone at the newspaper would want me to enter this thing?" I asked.

I knew that loose lips do sink ships and that hers were

among the loosest, but Joan felt warm and snugly against me, and I needed to talk to her about this. She was, after all, the only person inside the *Boston Patriot* with whom I felt safe. I could only hope that this would not be repeated over lunch with Lillian Gilmartin.

"What do you mean?"

"Crash Galovitch," I said. "He called and told me I should enter. He thought I had a chance."

"Public relations," Joan said. Joan had a quick mind. It was one of the things that attracted me to her.

"Public relations?"

"Sure," she said. "You know how black comedians can tell all these black stereotype jokes and nobody says they're racists?"

"Yes."

"Well, Molly's dead. People might criticize the *Patriot*, and say that the contest is in poor taste. But if they can show the world that Molly's closest friend entered the contest, that makes it okay. It's the same as saying that Molly would approve."

Of course, I thought. Joan was right. I had been used. Nobody wanted me to win this thing. They just wanted a letter of application from me. Look, they could say, waving my pathetic little letter, if Molly's friend didn't think this contest was an insult to her memory, why should anybody else?

Oddly, I felt relieved. My chance to get on *Lifestyles of the Rich and Famous* was dead, yes, and I did feel like a fool, but I was okay for now. I was not to be the ultimate sensitive male, but I was still determined to find my friend's killer.

And there was something else. Joan. What I felt for her was love, and it was a feeling I hadn't known for a while. More and more these idyllic Friday mornings felt to me like the early days of my marriage to Anne, those cloudy days when she and I had stayed in bed forever and read the papers.

I wanted to tell Joan what I was feeling, but I thought it would be cruel: "I love you, and by the way, this relationship has no future." So I said nothing. Soon Joan's hand was working its way between my legs and her thigh was pressing hard against mine. Her eyes, which had always seemed so serious or so sad, now sparkled with mischief.

"Dear Mr. Scotland," she whispered devilishly, "I want you. Signed, Horny at the Honeysuckle." She tickled my knees. It was something that Joan never would have done on our first visit to the Carefree Villa.

For so long I had been dreading the moment when I would have to clobber Joan with my rejection, have to tell her that I wasn't strong enough to take her away from her husband and her kid even if she wanted me to. And now, as a feeling of intense closeness swept over me, I suddenly had a vastly different problem. I didn't want to give her up.

She reached over now and turned off the lamp on her side of the bed. Then I turned off my lamp. We wrapped our arms and legs around each other and slid under the sheets. Soon our motion was tossing the pages of the newspapers to the floor.

At two o'clock I was back on Plum Island. It was a sunny February day, and I stopped first at the beach to walk on the sand and inhale the sea air, and try to figure out how I could get a job that would not make me feel like a trustee in some clean, well-lighted prison. Then I went to the drug store to pick up Rolaids. Guilt-induced stomach acids were roaring like Vesuvius just beneath my sternum. After that I drove to the post office to pick up my mail. As usual, I opened my mail in the post office so that I could deposit in the trash barrel the flyers from Sears, the pictures of famished children, and the computerized printout announcements that said I, Jeff Scotland, had won one of three fabulous prizes.

After I jettisoned the trash, I opened an envelope that looked as if it had a check in it. It did. Three hundred dollars from *Viewfinder* magazine for an article I had written about Sturbridge Village. The money was, to say the least, unexpected because the magazine had already paid me for the piece two weeks earlier. I pocketed the check, hoping they wouldn't catch their mistake.

The only other piece of mail was a letter from the *Boston Patriot.* I wasn't surprised. I had assumed they would send polite rejection letters to all the people who had entered. Probably something like "Thank you for your interest, but unfortunately your qualifications are not suited to our present needs."

I opened the letter.

"Dear Mr. Scotland," it began, "Congratulations. Out of more than 18,000 applicants you have been chosen as a semifinalist in our search for a new advice columnist."

CHAPTER 11

For a brief moment my adrenaline flowed like champagne. The dream was not dead after all. I could still become a nationally syndicated advice columnist, TV personality, rich person. I would be able to pay my bills and have safe sex with hundreds of women who didn't have husbands and kids. And of course catch Molly's murderer, too, Scotty, I rudely reminded myself, don't let that little thing slip your mind.

Before I left the post office, I read the rest of the letter and learned that there were 103 other semifinalists. So perhaps it was a wee bit early to go shopping for a mansion on Martha's Vineyard.

The letter, which was signed by Lawrence Dracut, said, "Enclosed are three letters that are typical of the kind Molly Collins has answered in recent years. We simply ask that you answer them. There are no further instructions, and no questions about the letters will be answered."

Oh, great, I thought. I had finished congratulating myself on being picked from the mire of 18,000 applicants, and now reality was showing its smug face again.

Sure, I had beaten out 18,000 dental assistants and data entry clerks, but now I was in the race with 103 qualified people. A hundred and three to one was practically hopeless. Even Hocus Pocus had gone off at 18–1. My chance of being the new "Dear Molly" was as thin as it had ever been, certainly not worth the time it would take to answer the sample letters and get rejected.

To make things more difficult the letters had to be returned to the *Boston Patriot* by the twenty-fourth of February, sent by registered mail, and postmarked no later than the twenty-third. It was already three o'clock in the afternoon on the twenty-third. Obviously the *Patriot* wanted someone who could write under the pressure of a deadline.

As I drove the few blocks back to the cottage, I resolved that I would not answer the letters. Earlier, with Joan, I had accepted the fact that I was out of the running, and I liked it that way. Maybe I was a failure, but at least I knew where I stood. I didn't want to get my hopes up again. And besides, if somebody was willing to kill for the job, was that really the kind of social set I wanted to get in with? There had to be safer ways of investigating Molly's murder than throwing myself blindly into the ring with the killer. As I pulled onto the gravel driveway in front of the cottage, I thought, even if I could answer the letters in time, I sure couldn't answer them cleverly enough to compete with a hundred and three other people who had also been plucked out of the mire. The fact that I was selected as a semifinalist would always be one of life's small victories, I thought, but nothing more.

Mungus was in his studio hunched over his drawing board. He was drawing a cartoon of two guys walking down a busy city street, and all the stores around them were named "ubiquitous." There was the Ubiquitous

Cleaners, the Ubiquitous Coffee Shop, the Ubiquitous Jewelry Store, and so forth. Mungus humor. I looked at Mungus's work and offered the appropriate nods of approval. I told him that I had arranged to get an interview with Lawrence Dracut. And then, without telling my friend that I had become a semifinalist, I slipped quietly into my office. I knew that if I told Mungus about the three letters, he would stalk my heels like a hound from hell until I had answered them and mailed them back to the *Patriot*.

In my office I pushed the "Dear So-And-So" letters into a manila folder so that I wouldn't be able to see them. I was curious about what was in the letters, but determined not to read them until the deadline was past. I sat at my desk, actively ignoring them. But my mind wandered to Molly.

"Dear Molly," I thought, *"I've been selected as a semifinalist in a contest, and if I were to win it, I could solve a lot of problems, as well as my friend's murder. But they want me to answer some letters, and I don't feel like it, because I know, with one hundred and three other finalists, I don't have a chance, so why bother. Signed, Baffled in Boston."*

"Dear Baffled," I heard Molly write back, *"Bullshit. You don't want to answer the letters because you're afraid of failing, afraid of succeeding, and afraid of getting your throat slit open. Stop whining and answer the letters."*

Okay, I thought, maybe it wouldn't hurt just to read the damn things. I pulled out the first letter. It said:

Dear So-and-So,
    You've heard of the *Hindenburg*? Well, I'm a blimp, too, and I feel as if I've crashed. I've hit bottom.

On my wedding day fifteen years ago I had a lovely figure and my weight was fine. I've had two kids since then and I eat out often. I also eat a lot of junk food when I'm nervous and depressed. The result of all this is that I'm thirty-seven years old and I weigh 215 pounds. I've gained a hundred pounds since my wedding day. I'm exhausted when I get to the top of a flight of stairs. I have to make my own clothes, kids stare at me on the street, and still I just keep eating. I've tried all the diets and I've signed up for lots of exercise classes. Once I lost thirty-five pounds but I put it all back on in three months.

Now my husband has given me an ultimatum. He says if I don't lose the hundred pounds within a year, he will leave me. He says he doesn't want to stand by and watch me kill myself. In a way I don't blame him. He doesn't find me attractive anymore, and we haven't had sex since last Easter. But I'm angry. He married me 'for better or worse,' didn't he? And besides, he's got plenty of flaws of his own. What should I do?

                                        Distraught in Des Moines

Even though I knew that the letters had been written by someone at the *Boston Patriot* and there was no "Distraught in Des Moines," I was touched by her letter. I remembered that my wife had once given me an ultimatum, too, and now that memory stabbed at me. "Get a real job," I remembered Anne saying, "because I'm not going to live like this for the rest of my life." "Like this" meant: in apartments, always owing money, driving old cars that broke down a lot.

I wrote five unpublished novels about sensitive young men during the years that Anne and I were together, and each one had seemed the answer to our prayers. With each we fooled ourselves into believing that this was the one that could sell big, get optioned for a movie, picked up by a book club, reprinted in paperback, make money. Then I turned to true crimes, and the first two did well, but the big money never really came. And with the McHale book's disastrous reviews, we began to slide back down the hill. Each year Anne seemed to age even more than I did, and what had once been a sunny, sassy relationship turned into something as bitter as bile. What was to become our triumph became my failure. The image of Anne saying, "Get a job, I'm not going to live like this for the rest of my life," now merged in my mind with a picture of her a year later actually walking out of the apartment, actually putting suitcases into the trunk of her car, actually driving away without a second look, even though I stood on the front steps and shouted "Utter failure, your ass," and then cried like a child.

I hadn't intended to write answers for any of these letters, but now I turned on the word processor and wrote:

Dear Desperate,

Hitting bottom hurts like the dickens, but at least it puts a foundation under you and leaves up as the only direction left to go.

Your husband's frustration is understandable and his motives might be good, but his ultimatum stinks. Ask him to replace it with "I love you, honey, and I will help you to lose weight." He did marry you for better or worse, and he owes you his support. But he also married you "till death do you part," and at 215 pounds you are hastening the day of parting.

If you are eating too much when you are nervous and depressed, you don't need to give up junk food.

You need to give up being nervous and depressed. A good counselor can help you with that. And get a doctor to put you on a realistic exercise program. Nobody ever lost a pound by "signing up" for an exercise class.

With all this outside support and your own determination, you can lose weight. You did it before. But don't use your husband's flaws as a reason to fail, and don't measure yourself against the way you looked fifteen years ago. We all looked a lot better then.

Love,
Scotty

After I printed the letter I reread it, wondering why on earth I had written it. Was it just the challenge? Or did I really think I could smash the competition, become a rich and famous advice columnist, and solve Molly's murder all in one motion? And what if there came a day when I could be the new Molly *or* bring her killer to justice, but not both? Which would I choose? I wondered.

I had an urge to mail the letter to Distraught in Des Moines, an urge frustrated by the fact that she was as fictitious as all those grateful clients I had counseled professionally in Albuquerque, New Mexico. Poor Distraught was probably the creation of a person who smoked cigars and cackled with scorn for her even as he invented her letter. Nevertheless, I felt bad for her.

Like puzzles needing to be solved, the other letters beckoned me. I read the next letter. It said:

Dear So-and-So,

Maybe I'm nuts, but I think my wife is playing around with my brother.

I don't have any real evidence, just a gut feeling.

Whenever Darren is around, Lana glows like a candle. She talks more, she tells jokes, she even walks differently, more feminine. I've always thought of our marriage as strong, but she's never been that flirtatious with me. During the last few months Lana has stayed out late at several "business-related dinners." Her job does require some socializing with clients, so I can't prove she's not having a harmless dinner, but it makes me wonder and worry.

We still have sex three or four times a week, so that part of our marriage seems okay. But I'm afraid.

I love Lana and I love my brother. I certainly don't want to accuse them if it's not true, but I don't want to be the chump who's the last to know. And if they are having an affair, then what? I don't think I could bear to see either one of them again. How do I resolve this dilemma?

Wondering in Waco

I was pleased that Wondering had not mentioned anything about a .357 Magnum and apparently had never followed his wife to a motel room. Wondering in Waco had never mentioned revenge at all. He had simply told me his feelings, and I felt bad for the guy. As I thought about his feelings, I recalled a time early in my marriage to Anne. We lived in a small apartment in Back Bay, and she was taking night courses at Boston University. One of her professors was a slick young Porsche-driving Southerner by the name of Christopher Horton, and I suspected that Anne was having an affair with him. She was taking a Wednesday night course in the literature of some misshapen European country, and it seemed as if all I heard over breakfast on Thursdays was "Chris this" and "Chris that." It made me so jealous that I could feel

my skin tighten whenever Anne mentioned his name.
Whining to my wife just because she thought her
professor was bright and charming seemed childish, so I
kept my silence. But the great lie detector between my
legs could not hide his limpness on those nights when
Anne came home late and I suspected she had been with
him. She knew something was wrong. My fears of losing
my wife burst from me halfway through one of those
long nights, and I had to wake Anne to tell her. I wanted
to talk about this Christopher Horton character, but
somehow in the darkness other things came out, moments with my mother, childhood rejections, dates I'd
never had in high school. Anne held me in her arms. By
dawn we were making love, and Anne assured me that
she loved only me. That midnight conversation widened
the avenue of communication between us, and the
months that followed were the happiest of our marriage.
Ironically, six years later, when Anne really did have an
affair, it annoyed me less than a case of food poisoning.
But to this day I cannot hear the name Christopher
without feeling scared.

To Wondering in Waco I wrote:

Dear Wondering,

The simple solution would be to invite your brother
over for a game of pinochle every time your wife has
one of those business-related dinners. If he continually
declines with curious excuses like "Gee, I'd love to,
but tonight I have to wash my parakeet," then perhaps
there is some basis for your fears.

But you said it yourself. There isn't any real
evidence. And "gut feelings" won't even get you an
audition on *Divorce Court*.

Lana might be more flirtatious with your brother

simply because he is your brother and that makes him safer than a dark-eyed professor or a stranger at the office, who might misunderstand.

You're not crazy. You're just a little insecure. It sounds as if you need more attention, not more evidence. Tell your wife. Don't let her be the last to know.

Love,
Scotty

"You slimy little cockroach," I heard Mungus say. "What the hell are you up to?"

As quietly as a lizard he had come into my office and planted himself behind me, where he was reading my letter.

"No big deal," I said, embarrassed that I hadn't told him about the letter from the *Patriot*. "I made the cut. I'm in the top one hundred and four for the 'Dear Molly' job."

"Way to go, Scotty!" Mungus shouted. He slapped my back. Then he snatched the letters off my desk and began reading. Inevitably he ended up tumbling onto my office couch. While he read I watched his face to see if he smiled often, to see how quickly his eyes moved, to see if he was anxious to get to the next page. Despite myself, I was taking pride in my letters.

"Hey, this is great stuff," Mungus said halfway through the second letter. "Graceland here I come."

"Look," I said, "before you start packing your guitar, I've got to tell you I'm not going any further with this thing."

"Are you out of your brain?" Mungus asked. "Why not?"

"Because, number one, I don't have a chance of

winning. And number two, the post office closes in ten minutes. And if the answers to these letters aren't sent by registered mail tonight, I'm history."

"Shit," Mungus said. "How many more letters do you have?"

"One," I said, glancing at the last, which I hadn't even read.

"Hey, no problem," Mungus said. "Let's get that little bugger up on the screen. I'll help you. I am, after all, your official assistant letter reader and all-around stooge."

"Mungus, there's no time."

"We've got ten minutes," Mungus said. He was off the couch now and pushing the final letter into my hand. "The post office is only a minute away." He glanced again at the letters he had read. "Jesus, these are good."

"Mungus, read my lips. There is no time."

"I'll get the envelope ready while you write something brilliant," he said.

"I haven't written anything brilliant in years," I said. "And even if I could, there's not enough time."

"So what you're saying is there's not enough time."

"Right, Mungus. You catch on real good."

"Okay, so screw brilliant. Just write something pretty good."

"We're talking about ten minutes," I said. "Subtract the time it takes to get into the post office before they lock the door and we're talking nine minutes. Two minutes to put the letter on the screen and a minute to print the letter, put in the envelope, and seal it. That leaves six minutes in which to be semibrilliant and correct my typing mistakes. N.F.T. Mungus. No Fucking Time."

Mungus stared at me as if he had known all along that I had mental problems.

"One twenty-seven to one twenty-six," he said.

"What?"

"One twenty-seven to one twenty-six," he said again.

"What the hell kind of gibberish is that?" I screamed. "I'm telling you there's no time and you're reciting arithmetic problems."

"One twenty-seven to one twenty-six," he said. "I should think those numbers would be etched in your memory. That was the final score of the Celtics-Lakers game, the one where the Celtics were down by ten with two minutes left and you said, and I quote, 'Those assholes don't have a chance now, there's not enough time.' And I said, 'Ten bucks says they win it,' and you said, 'You're on, asshole,' and they won it by one point, and the asshole turned out to be someone other than me."

I put the letter up on the screen. It said:

Dear So-And-So,

I'm eighty years old and my hearing is excellent, which is sometimes a curse. The other day I was on my bus and two teenage boys got behind me. They talked all the way, and it seemed to me that every other word was an obscenity. I don't think I've ever heard such a string of filth, even from the crazy street people who ride the bus. I have two teenage grandsons, and I would hate to think they talk like that.

Am I just an old fussbudget, or do today's teens really have filthy minds?

Shocked in Santa Cruz

It was six minutes to five. I read the letter to Mungus. "You'd better make it short," he said, "but be brilliant." By now he had addressed the envelope and slipped the other letters inside.

"I told you, I—"

"I know, I know, you haven't been brilliant for years. I'm just kidding. Write anything."

I stared at the words on the screen as if I'd never actually seen English before. For the first time ever, I could hear my watch ticking.

"So what are you going to tell her?" Mungus asked.

"I'm thinking, I'm thinking."

Mungus stood over me and leaned forward, as if by touching the computer screen with his nose, he could make the right words magically appear. I could smell the cologne on his cheeks, so I knew he must have a date with the bowling alley lady. I envied him. Maybe Mungus and the bowling alley lady would fall in love. Maybe they would get married and move to Elgin, Illinois, and I would grow old alone in this cottage.

"I'm blocked," I said. It was a feeling I hardly knew, of looking at words and being unable to respond to them.

"I'm blocked, too," Mungus said. "And I'm not even a writer."

My mind drifted to the only other time I could remember having writer's block. It was when I was writing an article about the use of lie detectors in business. I had talked to all the pro lie detector people about screening out white-collar criminals, protecting inventory from the nibbling of dishonest employees, saving the consumer money by reducing theft. And I had talked to all the anti lie detector people about invasion of privacy, misuse of the tool, incompetent testers, constitutional rights. And when it was time to write the article, I had stared at my typewriter as if it were a strange object from another galaxy. I couldn't write a word.

So I called up Molly and said, "Okay, Miss Great Advice, what have you got for a writer who is blocked?"

We talked about the problem and finally Molly gave her diagnosis. "You don't know how you feel about lie detectors," she said. "I know you, Scotland, and you can't write about an issue without knowing which side you are on. You have no place to write from. Figure out how you feel about lie detectors, then write."

Molly had been right, of course, and after three days of staring at a blank sheet of paper, I had decided that lie detectors sucked, and I wrote a pretty decent article.

"I don't want you to feel pressured or anything," Mungus was saying now, "but you've only got four minutes before the greatest opportunity of your life and mine vanishes forever."

I had wasted another minute thinking about writer's block.

"That's it," I said.

"That's what?"

"It's over," I said. "Time's up. I can't write an answer that fast, especially when I haven't even thought of what the answer is."

"Shit," Mungus said, and in the quiet that followed I could hear my watch ticking louder than before.

I put my head down and took a deep breath. I hated like hell to disappoint Mungus, but I knew that I wouldn't have had a chance, anyhow. For the third time that day I watched the "Dear Molly" job drift out of sight.

"I've got it," Mungus said. "Tell her yes."

"Tell who yes?"

"The old lady in the letter. Yes. That's your answer. Just 'Yes.'"

"But that doesn't make any sense," I said. "It doesn't answer her question. Yes, what? Yes, she's an old fussbudget, or yes, today's teens really have filthy minds?"

"What the hell's the difference," Mungus said, "as long as it gets a laugh?"

I wrote "Yes" and printed the letter. Mungus stuffed it in the envelope and rushed out the door, humming the tune to "Blue Suede Shoes."

CHAPTER 12

If Lawrence Dracut was a murderer, I would know it. I was sure. That's what I told myself when I got to Boston at nine o'clock on a morning in early March. I was scheduled to interview Dracut at ten.

I parked my car in the underground garage and walked along Boylston Street to the Boston Common. Then I strolled over to the Public Garden. These were places Molly and I had gone often. I bought a steaming cup of coffee from a pushcart vendor, then sat on a bench by the pond, pulling my coat around me to keep me warm.

As I watched people crisscross the Public Garden on their way to work, their breath visible in the cold air like little steam engines, I felt more alive than I had in months. I'd been cuckolded, abandoned, bereaved, and shot at. But today I was okay. I was excited about playing detective by doing this bogus interview with Dracut. I was even stimulated by the danger of investigating Molly's murder. And I was flattered and excited by my affair with Joan. Something was changing in me. I had, it seemed, some purpose in life.

From where I sat I could see most of the Boston

skyline projected around me. It's a lovely city, Boston, one that Molly loved more than all the cities that she jetted to on her speaking tours. Molly adored the changing of the seasons in Beantown. She knew every narrow cobblestoned alley, every musty old bookstore, every gossipy café in the city. Sad, I thought, that she will never see it again.

The pond, now drained for the winter, was an acre of mud, with here and there the sparkle of frost. But in spring and summer the swan boats would skate along the water, carrying tourists and lovers. The swan boats were a Boston tradition. And they were a Molly and Scotty tradition. Each spring we would come here and ride on one of the aging boats, which were pedaled in lazy circles around the pond by strong young college boys who sat behind huge antique swans.

Sitting on the bench on this chilled March morning, I couldn't remember ever riding on the swan boats with my wife, only with Molly. But we didn't do it last year, I thought regretfully. Or the year before.

Dear Molly, I thought, *What the hell happened to me? Why did I get so cynical? Was it because I had a little bit of fame and that son of a bitch Fred McHale took it away from me? Signed, Baffled in Boston.*

I sat and caressed my paper coffee cup to warm my fingers. I didn't really want an answer, but one came.

Dear Baffled, Molly said in my mind, *You got cynical because your dreams didn't come true. You wanted the perfect marriage, you wanted fame, you wanted children. But it wasn't McHale who took it all from you. Look inside yourself. It was you. The reviewers all agreed that your last book was a stinker, and they were right. You spent more time at the racetrack than you did researching that book. After the reviewers tore you apart, you were afraid to go through it again. You were afraid of becoming a well-known failure. McHale just made it easy for you to quit. Love, Molly.*

Molly was right. Look inside yourself for the answer. So I had looked inside myself and I'd come up with something I had to deal with. Fred McHale wasn't keeping me from success. Jeff Scotland was.

As I sat there sipping the hot coffee, I wondered what it was about today that allowed for such self-probing. At first I thought it was being in the Public Garden, sitting on a bench that, quite likely, I had once sat on with Molly. But it was something more, I realized, and I smiled when I understood. It was the letters. I had written those letters to "Distraught in Des Moines" and "Wondering in Waco," and they were good. For the first time in too long I had done something that I was really proud of, and maybe that made it safer to look at a few things that I was not so proud of.

As I walked out of the Public Garden, I tossed the remaining half of my coffee into a litter barrel, thinking half for me, and half for Dr. Lewis.

Fifteen minutes later I was in the parking lot of the *Boston Patriot* looking for Lawrence Dracut's parking spot. I discovered that Dracut drove a white Lincoln Town Car with a vanity plate that said DRACUT. I was sure that nobody would ever use such an identifiable vehicle for a deliberate hit-and-run, but I wrote down the information anyhow.

Dracut's office, which I entered a few minutes later, was the kind of room I had always dreamed of for myself. Almost everything in it was oak, green, brass, or leather. The furniture was dark, but sunlight poured in generously from a wide picture window. A painting of

Dracut's famous 1930 Cadillac hung on the wall beyond his desk, and two other walls were lined with shelves of leather-bound books that must have been worth even more than the Caddy.

Dracut rose from a great oak desk in the middle of the room and greeted me graciously. He was a middle-aged man . . . sixty, I had learned in my library research, and though he carried a few extra pounds, he moved athletically across the room.

"Mr. Scotland," he said, shaking my hand warmly. He had a round face, somewhat florid, and wise gray-green eyes. His brown beard was salted at the front and reddish on the sides. He directed me to a massive Chesterfield couch by the big window.

"It's been said that I make the finest cup of coffee in the state," he said. "Would you care for a cup?" Twenty-seven years in Boston had not diluted the rich accent he had brought with him from his home state of Tennessee. He was, to my great surprise, a charming man.

"Yes," I said. So much for Dr. Lewis.

He strode to a counter behind his desk and poured coffee into china cups from a tall silver urn while I found a socket for my tape recorder. "So," he said. "You're writing for *Glitz*. I've been watching that magazine. Very promising. Perhaps I'll buy it someday." He placed the cups on saucers, carefully brought the coffee across the room, and set it next to my tape recorder on the glass table by the couch. He smiled. "Of course, I won't buy it until after your story comes out. It wouldn't look good."

He sat beside me on the couch. Was this the sort of man who would kill just to squeeze more money out of a newspaper? I wondered.

I already knew a few things about Lawrence Dracut. He had made his first small fortune manufacturing boat trailers. Then he had started the extraordinary *Boston Lifestyles* magazine, a monthly that had no editorial content, only advertisements. The gimmick was that the magazine ran only extremely clever ads for unusual or high-priced items. Later Dracut had gone into sports posters and the financing of bright young entrepreneurs who had brains but no cash. Now he was into newspapers and there had been a lot of howling about that. The unions hated him and serious journalists thought he was a clown.

I popped a cassette into my tape recorder, realizing as I did that it didn't matter whether or not the tape came out. I didn't really have an assignment, except the one I had given myself, to catch Molly's murderer.

"So?" he said. "What shall we talk about?"

"The contest mostly," I said. "Why have one at all? Why not just hire somebody for the job?"

"It would take years to build up a new advice columnist to anything close to Molly Collins's popularity," he said. "And, to tell you the truth, it probably couldn't be done. But I figure if I have a contest, get lots of publicity, and announce that someone is the new Molly Collins, the papers will scoop her right up."

"Her?"

"Or him," Dracut said. "Man or woman, I don't care." He stared at the window, seeming to enjoy the feel of sunshine on his face.

"You know," he said thoughtfully, "it's amazing how much like sheep folks are."

"Huh?"

"You put suntan lotion in a bottle and call it Joe's Suntan Lotion and people won't buy it. But you put the exact same product in the bottle, change the label to

Coppertone and raise the price, and they'll scoop it right up."

"I didn't know you had been in the suntan oil business."

"I wasn't," Dracut said. He reached for his coffee. He had thick, workingman's hands. I knew that he had grown up poor, but he handled the china cup with great delicacy, as if he had been raised in a mansion. "I only mention the suntan lotion to make a point about the contest. The person who wins this thing is going to be the same person whether we call her Mary Smith or the new Molly Collins. But if we don't trumpet her as the new Molly Collins, nobody will read her column. People want Molly back. That's what this is all about. We can all pretend she's not dead."

"Sounds cynical," I said.

Dracut smiled. "George Bernard Shaw said that the power of accurate observation is commonly called cynicism by those who do not have it."

"Aren't you concerned that I'll print what you just said and your readers will think you take them for fools?"

"Not at all," he said. "My disdain for the great unwashed is well known. It just makes me more interesting to the public. It makes me a kind of brand name. Like Molly. See, people don't much care what you sell them, as long as they've heard of it."

"Are you going to pick the new Molly Collins?"

"Not alone," he said. "No, that wouldn't be right. I've got a committee. Two reporters, one minister, a psychiatrist. And me. We'll all read the letters."

"This contest," I said. "Is it indicative of your plans for the *Patriot*?"

Dracut smiled. "You're too polite, boy," he drawled. "What you mean is am I going to turn the *Patriot* into a gossip rag like the other papers that have fallen under my damnable influence?"

"Right," I said.

"Well, sure I am," Dracut said. "That's what I do. You can't change a man's nature just by giving him a fancy office." He swept his hands broadly through the air, indicating the fine surroundings. I wasn't sure if he was toying with me.

"You sound proud of it."

"Of course I am," Dracut said. "Honesty is always something to be proud of."

"Huh?"

"'An honest man is the noblest work of God,'" he went on. "Robert Burns. Now let me explain something to you about the newspaper business." Dracut leaned forward as he spoke, and he eyed the sensor light on my tape recorder to be sure it picked up every word. "This idea of news gathering being some kind of high-minded and noble profession is horseshit. That's a given. We're in the entertainment business and we're in business to make money."

"Well, there are some quality newspapers," I said.

"Really?" Dracut said. "I was not aware of that." He seemed genuinely surprised. "Well now, let me ask you this. Do you know of a newspaper that doesn't cover auto accidents if they're big enough and bloody enough? Have you heard of one that doesn't cover tragic fires in tenement houses if enough people are killed? Do you know of one that doesn't report the baseball scores and doesn't run interviews with the bimbo of the week?"

"No," I said.

"Well, there you have it. What does any of that stuff have to do with our lives? If a dozen people were killed in an early morning freeway pileup in California yesterday, you might enjoy knowing it, but it doesn't make a dime's worth of difference in your life, now does it. If the newspaper really wanted to keep you informed, it would print pieces on how to prevent fires instead of accounts of how six children were barbecued in a Louisville blaze, now wouldn't it. So we're all pandering to voyeurs. The only difference between me and the others is that I'm better at it." He sipped from his coffee cup. "And more honest about what I'm selling," he added.

"So you're saying that you print whatever people want to read."

He stared at me sympathetically. "Well, boy," he said, "I never went to Harvard Business School, or nothing like that, but it always seemed to me that that's what a good businessman does, creates a product that customers want to buy, not try to sell them what he thinks they should want."

We went on in that vein for a while. Dracut had a good deal to say, and he seemed to enjoy saying it.

"Was Molly Collins going to leave?" I asked when I was finally able to wrest the conversation from him.

"Why would she leave?" he asked. The question didn't seem to alarm him.

"Some people would prefer not to work for you," I said. "They don't share your disdain for the great unwashed."

"Well, let me put it this way," Dracut said. "If it came out that Molly was going to leave because she didn't want to work for me, that would not be the best publicity for the contest, so I wouldn't tell you."

"But that's not consistent with what you said a minute ago about letting the public think what they want of you."

"'A foolish consistency is the hobgoblin of small minds,'" Dracut said.

"Longfellow," I said.

"Emerson," he corrected. "But I'll tell you what. Can I talk to you off the record?"

"Sure," I said. I reached over and turned off the tape recorder.

"Yes, she talked about leaving," he said. His trust in me was surprising. "When Miss Collins heard I was taking over the paper, she got hot enough to burn a wet mule. She was a woman of principle, and she said her principles didn't allow her to work for me. That's fine. She was wrong, of course, but a person has a right to be wrong. Anyhow, she came to me snorting and whining about journalistic integrity and all that. We talked it out. I told her she was free to disassociate herself with me in public and she would still have complete control over her column. She knew I was a man of my word, and eventually saw the wisdom of what I was saying, as people invariably do, and she agreed to stay."

"Would you have had the contest if she left, but hadn't died?"

Dracut leaned back, stroked his beard, thought it over.

"No," he said. "In ten years the advice column will be a relic. It works now if you've got a brand name, a 'Dear Abby,' or an Ann Landers, or a Molly Collins. Or, if you can link someone new with the brand name, which is what we're trying to do here. But I doubt that there will be any new big names in advice columns. It wouldn't be worth it to try to build one up."

For a long time we talked about advice columns. We went over some of the history I had covered with Lillian Gilmartin. We talked more about the contest. Dracut seemed amused by the idea that a factory worker from

Missouri could soon be advising millions of people on how to handle their stepchildren. While we talked I studied the office, and I saw that on one corner of Dracut's desk there was a large ring of keys. He must have a key to every office in the building, I thought.

The conversation wound down and I had no more clever questions to ask. He offered more coffee and I declined. I told him I was almost done.

"Just a few more things," I said. "Personal stuff. Any hobbies?"

"I play a little golf," he said. "Some chess."

"Hunting?" I said.

"No. I used to hunt with my daddy when I was a boy. Didn't enjoy killing things. I do a little shooting, though."

"Rifles?" I asked. If Dracut was the man who shot up Mungus's cottage, then the question was freighted with meaning. I looked for some reaction.

"Handguns," Dracut said, looking me straight in the eye.

"Are you a good shot?"

He smiled. "Does a cat have an ass?" he said.

I packed my notes and tape recorder into my briefcase, but deliberately let my tape recorder cord fall into the crack between cushions on the couch.

We stood up. "Anything you want to add to this?" I asked.

"Just one thing," Dracut said. "If you ask around about me, you will hear that I cheat on my wife. I would not care to see that rumor in print. My wife is a fine woman, and she would be hurt and embarrassed by such an accusation." He pointed to a photograph on his desk. His wife was a gray-haired lady, seemingly older than him, with a warm, but somewhat maternal, face. She looked like a woman who could bake a great pie, but wouldn't know what to grab on to in bed.

"Is it true?" I asked. "Do you cheat on your wife?"

"Of course not," Dracut said with a grin. "Of course not."

In fact, I had heard the rumor from Joan and Brem Hyde that Dracut made a lot of unnecessary "business trips," and probably had some honey out of town. But that was not the sort of thing I would have put in an article even if I were really writing an article.

I knew that Dracut would show me to the elevator. He was that sort of man. We got outside his office, and as soon as he pushed the button for the elevator, I said, "Oh, forgot my cord," and rushed back into his office while he waited for the elevator. First I went to his desk. I took the ring of keys and shoved them into my briefcase. Then I grabbed my cord from the couch and carried it out to the elevator.

"Got it," I said.

CHAPTER 13

"Hot enough to burn a wet mule?" I said to Mungus. "Can you believe that?" It was a few minutes after two o'clock in the morning. We were sitting in my car, parked across the street from the *Patriot* building. "And Dracut said Molly was snorting and whining. He made it sound as if she just lost her temper. Did you ever know Molly to lose her temper?"

"Molly never lost her temper," Mungus said. Pressed against his eyes were an expensive pair of Swiss binoculars. Through the binoculars Mungus watched the main entrance to the *Patriot* building. "She was as cool as a trout's tit."

Like an old married couple, Mungus and I tended to have every conversation nineteen times. This was the third or fourth replay of this one. At the cottage I had told Mungus that I had stolen Dracut's keys, so that we could snoop around in the *Patriot* building. For one thing, I wanted to see the purchase requisition for the *USA Today* ad space. I wanted to know if the space had been reserved before or after Molly died.

We had been parked there since midnight. It had been

quiet, though now and then a cab would come by, rattling over the potholes, or we would hear the wailing of a distant drunk. It was also chilly, so periodically I had turned on the engine and run the heater full blast.

From the car Mungus and I could track the movements of the night security guard, whose desk was bathed in light behind the wide glass double doors at the entrance to the building. I held a notebook on my lap to record the guard's rounds. Mungus and I wore sports jackets and neckties. My idea. That way, if a police car pulled up, we could pass ourselves off as respectable men and say that we were waiting to pick up a reporter on the graveyard shift.

"So Dracut was blowing smoke up my ass," I said.

"Right."

"The question is, why."

"Hold it," Mungus said. "There goes Captain America on rounds." For no apparent reason, during the two hours we had been keeping track of the guard's rounds, Mungus had called the guard "Captain America."

I checked my watch. It was ten past two. The guard had gone on rounds at ten past midnight, and ten past one. Each time, he had arrived back at his desk in the lobby fifteen minutes before the hour.

"Okay," I said. "We go in at ten past three." Though Mungus had been reluctant to join this little expedition, it was he who had explained to me that the security guard would have a set pattern of rounds, because he had to plug his security clock into certain checkpoints every hour. Mungus had once been a security guard at Raytheon for three days.

It had been easy to follow Captain America's movement through the building. When he got to a floor, lights would go on. When he left, lights would go off. Only the fourth floor, fully lit, was exempt from this pattern. The fourth floor was the editorial department, and there would be a handful of graveyard reporters in and out all night. After my visit with Dracut the previous morning, I had roamed around the building to see where things were. Now I was hoping that we wouldn't have to go to the fourth floor, that we could find what I wanted in the purchasing department, on the second floor.

"Why would Dracut do that?" Mungus said. He put the binoculars down and began to unwrap the second of two submarine sandwiches he had bought at the Trolley Stop delicatessen for the stakeout.

"Do what?"

"Blow smoke up your ass."

"Because he's got something to hide," I said.

"Right," Mungus said. "So you stole his keys."

"It was an impulse," I said. "I told you that. They were there, that's all."

"Like Mount Everest."

"Yes."

"So, let me see if I've got this," Mungus said. "Dracut is blowing smoke up your ass, and that's why you've got me involved in this Watergate-type break-in."

It had taken me hours to get Mungus in on this caper and now I could sense that his feet were getting cold, figuratively as well as literally.

"Molly was your friend, too," I said. "Besides, we're not breaking in. I've got keys. I just wouldn't want the guard to see me fumbling with them because I don't know which key is the right one."

"And you wouldn't want him to see that you don't have an employee identification badge," Mungus said.

"Yes."

"Because he might think that you stole the keys, which you did."

"Right," I said.

"But other than that," Mungus said, "this is all perfectly kosher."

"Right," I said. "If you get caught you can say that you didn't know I stole the keys."

"Good," Mungus said. "I'm positive that everybody will believe that. It has such a ring of truth about it. Look, Scotty, I'd really love to burglarize this building with you, but, you see, I have this thing about being raped in jail by guys name Bruno, so perhaps I should just wait in the car for you."

"Mungus," I said, "I thought you wanted to be my stooge?"

"That's after you're rich and famous," he said.

"Well, this is your chance to prove you're a good stooge," I said.

"You're positive we won't get caught?"

"Positive," I said. "Besides, even if the guard sees us, which he won't, we'll just tell him we're a couple of reporters who normally work the day shift."

"I don't know," Mungus said.

"And there is one other little reason you should do this," I said.

"What's that?"

"Well, it's so trivial I almost hate to bring it up."

"Bring it up," Mungus said.

"Well, see if you can follow me on this. If we don't catch Molly's killer, then he could come back and shoot at us again and this time the bullet could crash into your skull and lodge in your brain and kill you, or leave you paralyzed from the waist down for life."

"I see," Mungus said.

At quarter to three the security guard was back at his desk. Mungus had eaten his sandwich and now he was sleeping. At ten past three I picked up the binoculars and watched as the guard put away his paperback book, picked up his clock, and left his desk to go on rounds. I woke Mungus. "It's time," I said.

With Lawrence Dracut's collection of keys clutched in my hand, and a flashlight tucked into my back pocket, I got out of my car quietly and dashed across the Street, in a manner which can best be described as furtive.

"Wait up, Scotty," I heard Mungus call, "I want to get arrested, too."

Mungus got out of the car and hung back in the middle of the street, where he could look up at the windows and watch the lights go on, while I fiddled with one key after another.

"The guard's on the second floor," he said. "Of course, a reporter could come to the door anytime now and call the police. But don't let that bother you."

"I've got it," I said as I twisted a key and felt the bar lock come up. We hurried in and locked the door behind us.

Mungus and I, crouching for no logical reason, moved the way we thought cat burglars would, along the lighted first-floor corridor to the stairs behind the bank of elevators. The building smelled of Pine Sol, and our careful steps seemed to echo like rocks falling into a canyon. The floors had been recently washed, and with the precious paranoia of the wrongdoer, I worried that Mungus and I would leave traceable footprints.

At the bottom of the stairs we found our first puddle of semidarkness. There we pressed our backs to the cool stone wall and stared up at the sliver of light that glinted under the crack of the second-floor fire door. When that light went out, it would mean that Captain America was moving on to the third floor.

"You're sure that the president approved this," Mungus whispered.

After five minutes the light went out. Mungus and I moved stealthily up the stairs. At the top step we paused and took a deep breath. "I wonder how much jail time G. Gordon Liddy did?" Mungus said. I pushed open the door with my fingertips, and we entered the darkness of the second floor. In the darkness it was easy to imagine the sounds of people coming. I thought I could hear the wailing of a police siren in the distance, and of pistols coming out of their holsters.

"Where's purchasing?" Mungus whispered.

"I've got to think," I whispered back.

"What do you mean you've got to think? I thought you cased this place this morning."

"I did," I said. "But I did it from the elevator. Now I've got to reverse everything in my mind."

After a minute I decided that we should turn left. I aimed my flashlight ahead of us. Mungus and I crept quietly down the corridor, stopping to shine the beam on the stenciled signs on each office door.

The fifth office that Mungus and I came to was the purchasing department. We stopped. I twisted the door-knob, half expecting to trigger an explosion of flashing lights and shrieking alarms.

"It's locked," I whispered. I handed the flashlight to Mungus while I fumbled again with the numerous keys. In the dark corridor their tinkling sounded like a forty-piece orchestra.

The key that was third from the end was the one that worked. Mungus and I pushed open the office door and edged ourselves into the purchasing office. There were tall windows across from us, and the lights from the street bounced a patchwork of shadows onto the office walls. Would the file cabinet also be locked? I wondered. And what were the chances that a key to a file cabinet in the purchasing department would be on Dracut's key ring?

I cast my flashlight beam about the office like a fishing line. There, in the corner by the windows, was a formidable metal file cabinet. "We might need a crowbar," I said to Mungus.

"A crowbar? Where the hell are we going to get a crowbar? I've never even seen a crowbar," Mungus said. "Now that I think of it, what the hell is a crowbar, anyhow?"

We stumbled and bumped our way across the office. When we got to the file cabinets, we froze like mannequins and listened again for the sounds of the building. Then Mungus crept over to the window.

"Captain America is still on the third floor," he said.

"How do you know?"

"The lights are reflected in the building across the street."

"Are you sure you haven't done this before?" I said.

The file cabinet was unlocked. I pulled open the top drawer and it squeaked like a rusty hinge. I whispered the *F* word, then aimed my flashlight into the drawer. The files, contained in manila folders, were arranged alphabetically by vendor. This one went *A* to *G*. I closed it. In the third squeaky drawer I found a file marked USA TODAY.

"This is it," I said. I could feel adrenaline careening through my system. I was sure I was about to make some great discovery. Mungus moved to the door and opened it a crack so that he could listen for intruders.

In the *USA Today* file I found what I was looking for. On October eighth, ten days before Molly died, a purchase order had been sent to *USA Today* reserving a full page of advertising space in the November fifteenth edition.

"That's it," I said out loud.

"What?" Mungus asked in a stage whisper.

"They reserved the ad space before Molly died."

"Who?"

"The *Patriot*," I said. "The purchasing agent. They were planning the contest while Molly was still alive."

Mungus tiptoed over to me now. He grabbed my shoulder. In the eerie reflected light of the flashlight I could see both fear and pride in his face.

"Then she really was murdered," he said. "This proves it. They murdered her so they could sell the new Molly Collins."

"Yes," I said. "That is, if Dracut was telling the truth about Molly agreeing to stay with the paper. How else could they plan on her being gone?"

It made sense, and yet it made no sense at all. And that troubled me. If Molly was staying with the *Patriot*, what would be the point of killing her? And did they really think they could kill Molly in October and advertise for her replacement in November? It would be in poor taste, to say the least. And besides, no ad had ever appeared in November.

I looked beneath the purchase order. The next item was a letter to *USA Today*, dated October twentieth, two days after Molly's death. The letter, signed by the *Patriot*'s purchasing agent, canceled the November fifteenth ad space and reserved a full page in the February ninth edition, which was the day I went to Dr. Lewis, the day when the announcement about the contest actually ran.

"Shit," I said. I showed Mungus the letter. "Now I'm confused. It looks as if Molly's death really did take them by surprise."

"Them" and "they," I thought, while Mungus looked at the letter. Somehow Molly's death was too monstrous to have been carried out by a simple "he" or "she." But, of course, I knew that there was no great conspiracy to kill Molly Collins. Just a single small person.

"What do we do now?" Mungus asked.

"We go upstairs."

"Upstairs?"

"To Molly's office," I said.

"It's a small point," Mungus said a few minutes later, after we had locked the purchasing office door and followed the beam of my flashlight up the stairs to the fourth floor, "but it seems to me you said there would be reporters working all night on the fourth floor."

"That's correct," I said. "So we have to be clever. We can't sneak into Molly's office. We have to make it look as if we're supposed to be there."

"In order not to wake up in jail tomorrow morning, is that right, Scotty?"

"That's right," I said.

It was three-thirty when we stood on the fourth floor landing. We decided to wait until 3:45, when the security guard would be back at his desk in the front lobby. We crouched in the dark at the top of the stairs and tried to come up with clever ideas for getting into Molly's office without getting caught. At 3:40 Mungus said, "I've got it. These neckties. Who the hell wears neckties?"

"Losers?" I said.

"No," he said. "Cops."

At 3:45 we came through the fire door and walked around the elevator bank into the lighted corridor. There was a small square window on the door to the city room. We peeked through it to see what we were getting into. There were two young women reporters working at VDTs near the front of the room and two men shooting the breeze over by the coffee machine on the far side. All of them were in their twenties. The entire room was fluorescently lighted and the surface of every desk was cluttered with papers, as if it were the middle of the day, and everybody was out to lunch.

"Okay," Mungus said, "follow me."

He opened the door and walked confidently in. I trailed him. Mungus called across the room to one of the guys having coffee, "Hey, pal, can you help me out here? Which one of these offices belonged to Molly Collins? You know, the advice lady?"

All of the reporters looked at Mungus. He was much too big to ignore. The guys who were drinking coffee acted as if they had been caught at something. One of them pointed to Molly's office and began moving back toward his desk.

The other one, an eager carrot-head with a spiral notebook in his hand, came over to us.

"What's up?" he said.

"Bomb threat," Mungus explained.

"Bomb threat?"

The reporter started patting at his pockets, looking for a pen.

"Yes," Mungus said. "Some psycho says he's going to level the building unless you call off the 'Dear Molly' contest. Says you're desecrating the name. Can you beat that."

"Jesus," the reporter said. He grabbed a pen from the

nearest desk and began scribbling. "And you are?" he said.

"Detective Stiles," Mungus said. "That's Stiles with an *i*. This is Detective Murdock. Now Murdock here is going to have to go through the files in Ms. Collins's office to see if we can't find the name of this looney who's been threatening to blow the place up. I'm going to have to search the area. I could use your help."

"Sure," the reporter said as he continued scribbling furiously.

Mungus grabbed Dracut's key chain out of my hand and dangled it in front of the reporter. "We got these keys from security," he said. "Trouble is, we don't know which one goes to Ms. Collins's office. Can you help us?"

"Sorry," the reporter said. Mungus shrugged and handed the keys back to me.

I went to Molly's door and fumbled with the keys until I found the right one. I could hear Mungus saying to the reporters, "We're going to have to make a visual inspection of every desk in the room. If you see any boxes or bags that don't look kosher, give a holler. Don't touch anything, or we could all be on the first floor in seconds. We got guys who get paid for handling bombs."

It was startling to step into Molly's office in the middle of the night. I felt as if I were walking on her grave. I suddenly wanted to turn back, forget the whole thing, let it rest, let Molly rest. Instead I took a deep breath, switched on an overhead light, and went to the file cabinet. Molly was here, I thought. She existed. She was my friend. And now she doesn't exist.

It seemed to me that if Molly had planned to leave the *Boston Patriot* for another newspaper, some evidence of

it would have to show up in her files. So I went through
them alphabetically.

There was a lot to go through. There were letters from
the Burlington Haddasah and the Bristol County Com-
municators asking Molly to speak at their annual meet-
ings. There were letters from Molly explaining why she
couldn't speak on those dates. And there were letters
accepting invitations. And letters to radio stations saying,
yes, she'd be glad to do a call-in show, or no, she
wouldn't be able to appear, and there was a letter from a
soup company asking her to endorse their cream of
chicken. There were no letters from advice seekers.
Those letters, hundreds of thousands of them, had to be
incinerated from time to time because they were confi-
dential and because they took up too much room.

Under *L* for *Lansky* I found it. A letter from Molly to
Arnold Lansky, the former publisher of the *Patriot*. The
letter was dated October third.

"Dear Arnold," it said, "This is just to put on paper
some of what we discussed this morning. As you know,
my contract with the *Patriot* allows me to resign if the
newspaper is sold. Since the *Patriot* has been sold to a
man who has no journalistic integrity, I have decided to
exercise that option. It has, of course, been a joy to work
with you these many years, and I will always be grateful
for the encouragement and the opportunity which you
gave me. My attorney will be in touch with you and with
Mr. Dracut to work out the details of my leaving. Love,
always, Molly."

There were more letters in the file. Most of them were
copies of faxes from Molly's lawyer to Lansky and
Dracut, clarifying the syndication deal. Whichever newspaper Molly went to would have to offer her column first
to the newspapers that were already buying it from the

Patriot, except in cities where Molly's new employer already had an affiliate newspaper. As near as I could read between the lines of the legalese, this wouldn't cushion the financial blow to Dracut, but would help him keep good relations with the newspapers who were buying his syndication package.

But all the legal mumbo jumbo did prove beyond doubt that Molly had resigned from the *Patriot* and was planning to take the "Dear Molly" column to another newspaper. I stuffed the entire file under my sports jacket.

Before I closed the file drawer, I spotted a file marked SCOTTY. I didn't want to look at it, but I couldn't stop myself. It was a thick manila folder, and in it were all the funny little cards I had sent Molly at work over the years, the thank-you notes, the cartoons I had clipped out of magazines. These were my love letters to Molly, I thought. I took that file, too.

"Detective Murdock," I called to Mungus, who was still poking around in desks at the front of the room. He gave me a look, then came rushing up to me. "Stiles," he whispered. *"You're* Murdock."

"Oh. Sorry. Have you completed your search?"

"Yes," he said loudly. "This place is clean." Then he called the reporters together. "You can go back to work," he told them. "Sorry for the inconvenience, but we have to take these things seriously. If anything comes up, give me a call at the station."

And we were off. We snuck downstairs to Lawrence Dracut's office on the third floor. Mungus held the flashlight while I found the key to Dracut's office. When we got inside, we didn't even need the flashlight. The reflected light from the street came through the window by the couch where Dracut and I had talked. From

Dracut's key chain I removed the key to the front door, which would get us out of the building. I easily found my way to the leather couch and tossed the rest of the keys under it, figuring sooner or later Dracut would find them. It was five minutes past four o'clock in the morning.

Mungus and I waited on the third-floor landing until ten past. Then we dashed down the two flights of stairs, through the lobby, out the door, across the street, and into the car, laughing all the way like a couple of young boys who had gotten away with something.

"What did you find out?" Mungus asked me when we finally stopped laughing.

"That Lawrence Dracut has something to hide," I said.

CHAPTER 14

I didn't sleep.

At nine o'clock that same morning I drove back to Boston, parked illegally in front of the *Patriot* building, took the elevator up to the third floor, rushed past Dracut's secretary, and rushed into Dracut's office. I was mad as hell.

"Mr. Scotland," Lawrence Dracut said, looking up from his desk. "I wasn't aware that we had another appointment this morning."

"Don't be so polite," I said. "I've barged in."

"Is there something you want?" he asked.

Sitting there with his collar open, Dracut wore an expensive suede jacket and a Rolex watch that cost more than my car. He looked as confident as one of those characters in a James Bond movie who, if the need arose, could push a secret button that would drop me into a pool of piranha fish.

"Why did you tell me that Molly was staying with the *Patriot*?" I asked. "She wasn't staying. She resigned."

"Who told you that?" he asked. Those wise eyes of his seemed to shine with admiration. Dracut seemed to think more of me because I was able to find out that he had lied to me.

"It doesn't matter who told me."

"Of course not," he said. "It's just that few people knew."

"So why did you lie?"

"I told you yesterday," he said. "It would not be good publicity for the contest if the public thought Molly was less than happy here."

"So what was all that 'off the record' bullshit? Why not just lie to me in the first place?"

"It's been said that you were once a good reporter. True crime books, I understand. You might not have believed me if the answer came too easily. I find that if I take someone into my confidence when I don't have to, it never occurs to them that I'm lying. Apparently, not this time."

"Apparently," I said.

"Still," Dracut said. "I'm not sure why this has you so churned up. You come in here sounding like a hen that's just laid an ostrich egg."

"I think you murdered Molly Collins," I said.

Now Dracut stood, as a precaution. For quite a long time he stared at me, sizing me up.

"Molly was hit by a car," he said softly, as if he were breaking the news to me.

"It was murder," I said.

Dracut sat down again. His fingers played nervously on the green blotter that covered much of his desk. I moved closer and stood glaring at him. He looked at me, without speaking, his eyes asking me to continue. So I told him about the message on my answering machine, the shooting at the cottage, my friendship with Molly.

"And you think I did it?" Dracut said when I was done.

He didn't try to talk me out of the idea that Molly had been murdered.

"Yes."

"Why would I?"

"For money. For the contest. Who the hell would be interested in running the new Molly Collins if they could have the old Molly Collins?"

"Probably nobody," Dracut said. "You're right about that."

He pressed his hand against his chin and thought hard. He seemed to be truly troubled by the idea of Molly being murdered. Watch it, Scotty, I thought, he's working on you again.

After a minute Dracut rose again from his leather chair. This time he walked around to the side of the desk, where there was a hammered copper wastebasket, slickly polished and bright as a new penny. He picked it up and emptied its contents, a few pieces of paper, onto the carpet. Then he cleared away a few papers from the middle of his desk and placed the wastebasket there.

He reached into the pocket of his corduroy trousers, pulled out his wallet, and removed five one-hundred-dollar bills. He waved them at me. Good God, I thought, is he going to try to bribe me with five hundred bucks?

"Let me show you something," he said. He went around to the front of his desk, and from the top drawer he removed a small elegant pipe lighter. He lit the bills on fire and dropped them into the wastebasket.

"What the hell are you doing?" I asked. I could feel the heat from the burning money against my face.

"Making a point," he said. He looked around, somewhat smugly, as if there might be television cameras catching all of this. Then he glanced into the wastebasket. "That's what I think of money, boy."

"Huh?"

He stared into the wastebasket and waited for the money to burn completely.

"Sit down," he said. I sat down.

He moved to the sideboard. "Coffee?" he asked.

"No."

He poured himself coffee. Then he put the wastebasket back on the floor, poured the trash back into it, and sat behind his desk contentedly sipping coffee from a china cup.

"Mr. Scotland," he said. "What I have just burned in that wastebasket are green pieces of paper, nothing more. I must have, I don't know, maybe eighteen million dollars of my own. I earn another two million a year just in interest. That's a pretty tall stack of green paper, now isn't it? I'm sixty years old, and if I live to be a hundred and four, which I intend to do, I'll still never get to the bottom of that stack. I've met a man or two I wouldn't mind killing in my time. But I would never kill a person just so I could add some money to the bottom of my stack, money I would never get to spend. And I especially would never kill a lady. I'm much too fond of the ladies."

"Then why run a contest at all, if not to make money?" I asked. "For that matter, why buy newspapers or anything else?"

"Why play golf or tennis?" he said.

"Huh?"

"Business is a game," Dracut explained. "Like everything else we do, it's a game we play to keep our minds off the fact that we are doomed to eternal oblivion. It happens to be a game that I enjoy playing, just as I enjoy a good game of poker. I try to make money because that's how you keep score."

What could I do? I just sat there. I didn't know whether I had been proved an idiot, or charmed into submission. "I guess I will have some coffee," I said. I was stalling. I had no idea of what to say next. I stood to move toward the coffee.

"I'll fetch it," Dracut said in that gracious southern way of his.

In a moment he gently placed a cup of coffee on a saucer into my hands along with a napkin.

"So," he said, back at his desk. "Now that we've got that straightened out, I've got an idea. How would you like to make five thousand dollars?"

Here it comes, I thought, the bribe.

Dracut raised a hand in front of him and ran it through the air as if he were setting a headline in type. It reminded me of Dr. Lewis planning his career as an advice columnist.

" 'My Search for Molly Collins's Killer,' " he said, "by her closest friend. Yes, I like it a lot. We won't run it until after we've chosen her replacement, of course. It will boost interest in the new column."

"No," I said. But in the back of my mind I was thinking: five thousand dollars. That would pay off a lot of the bills that were stacked in a wicker basket under my desk at home.

"Okay," Dracut said easily. "I'm not a man to push people into things they don't want to do."

He sipped his coffee and returned his attention to some papers on his desk. Then he looked up. "I believe your business here is done," he said. Finally he was showing the anger that he had been feeling all along. He was insulted that I had accused him of murder. Or was this new harshness in his voice just one more bet in a poker game?

When I got to the door, he said, "By the way, Mr. Scotland, congratulations."

"How's that?"

"The contest," he said. "You made the final seven."

"You knew I was in the contest?" I said.

"Not until this morning. My secretary removed all the names from the letters and coded them before we read them. We didn't know if they were written by males or females, friends or foes. Needless to say, I was surprised to see that several of us, including me, had picked you as a finalist. I hope you'll be available for the publicity we've got planned."

"I guess after today my chances of winning have gone down the tube," I said.

Again Dracut seemed to be insulted.

"Your chances of winning are as good as they have ever been," he said sternly. "If liking me were a job requirement around here, half my employees would have to leave. I've always made it my practice to hire the best people for the job regardless of what they think of me personally." He paused. "Or what I think of them. That's why I've been successful. Ability is what counts if you want to win the game, not sentiment. Of course, if you'd rather not work for an alleged murderer, we could take your name out of the running."

He stared right at me. Clearly, he was enjoying this. Is this a game, too? I wondered. Is everything a game? If this was a game, he had just made a winning move.

"No," I said sheepishly. "I'd like to stay in the contest."

"Fine," he said, "fine. Have a nice day, boy."

CHAPTER 15

Oprah Winfrey, microphone in hand, stood in front of me and paced back and forth, waiting for her cue. I sat in the Chicago television studio with the other Molly finalists, two men and four women, each of us in an orange swivel chair, spaced evenly across a small stage. In front of us was Oprah's live audience, smaller than it looks on TV, composed mostly of women. And, aimed at us from three directions, were the television cameras that would bring us into millions of living rooms.

Then the show began and Oprah explained about the contest, in case anybody had been in Cambodia and hadn't heard about it.

"Our first finalist in the search for a new Molly Collins is the Reverend Frank Cheetham," Oprah said, reading from notes that had been handed to her just before the show. "Reverend Cheetham is an outspoken supporter of the feminist movement. He is the author of *How to Stop Whining and Get On with Your Life,* and three other self-help books. He's from Los Angeles and he has two daughters."

It had been two weeks since Lawrence Dracut had told me that I was a finalist. A lot had happened since. The names of the seven finalists had gone out over the Associated Press wire that day. That night our photos were on CNN and Headline News, and the next day we were in all the newspapers. *USA Today* ran photos and short bios, culled from our application letters. Even the *New York Times* and *The Wall Street Journal* took note of the contest.

Twenty-four hours later I flew to New York to appear on David Letterman's show. Somehow Letterman's producers had sensed that, out of all the contestants, I was the one who would be willing to answer letters that had supposedly been written by pets, pieces of furniture, and food products.

Some of the other finalists showed up on *Good Morning America* and *Live with Regis and Kathy Lee*. Geraldo wanted us all, but his people called Crash and canceled when they found out we had Oprah on our dance card. Now we were all on tour, appearing on local and syndicated TV shows. Just as Hattie Slater had predicted, the *Patriot* was going to wring every last ounce of publicity out of this search for the new Molly Collins.

"Our next finalist is Jean Stone of Springfield, Illinois," Oprah said. "Jean is a former gymnastics champion who now counsels unwed mothers. She is married to a casino operator and has seven children."

As I waited for Oprah to get to me, I was nervous. But I wasn't nervous about being in the spotlight. In fact, I was getting used to that. Ever since the finalists had been announced, I'd become, at least on Plum Island, as easy to spot as a Yellow Cab. During the first three days I had appeared in local newspapers and on every Boston talk show. Strangers had stopped me on the street and asked me for my advice, and they seemed as happy as pups when I took the time to give it to them. If Mungus and I went into a local restaurant and I was not recognized, Mungus would fix that by telling everybody who I was. Though I was new to Plum Island, they all treated me like their local boy who made good. Back at the cottage, Mungus spent a lot of time singing "Don't Be Cruel," and "Love Me Tender."

No, being seen on television didn't scare me, I thought. In fact, I thrived on the attention and I loved sleeping in luxurious hotel rooms, even if I did spend much of the night wishing that Joan could be with me. What did trouble me was that every time the camera came on, and every time a reporter pulled out his notebook or thrust a microphone in front of me, I was haunted by three sentences. The first sentence was "For three years I worked as a Licensed Independent Clinical Social Worker in private practice in Albuquerque, New Mexico." The second sentence was "I specialized in personal and family counseling." And the third sentence was "I am a member of the American Association for Marriage and Family Therapy." Those lines from my letter ran through my mind constantly while we seven toured. With all this publicity I was bound to be unmasked, I thought. People would say my name in the same breath with Clifford Irving, Gary Hart, Richard Nixon, and Tawana Brawley. Of course I would be caught. What about Ted Schlagel, the black gynecologist from Arizona, who was also a finalist? Surely, he would be on to me. Those southwestern states were right next to each other. He probably knew every therapist in New Mexico and would spot me as a fraud.

"The next finalist I want you to meet is Jill Levinson from Lexington, Kentucky," Oprah said. "Jill is an interior decorator and a children's entertainer. She is the hostess of *The Story Princess,* television show, which is broadcast all over Kentucky and Ohio. Welcome, Jill."

I looked at Jill Levinson as she smiled into the camera. She was a short, dark-haired beauty, adorable. Like the others, she looked innocent and excited and just thrilled that she had been picked out of eighteen thousand. If she wins this contest, she, *The Story Princess,* will be the beneficiary of Molly's death, I thought. Was there any way she could have taken time out from her tales of billy goats and frightened piggies to arrange for all this to happen? I looked at the others, each somewhat tense in the glare of studio lights, and asked myself the same question. And then it crossed my mind, not for the first time, that if I won I would be the beneficiary of Molly's death. It was an uncomfortable thought. I tried to push all thoughts of Molly aside, but the next finalist that Oprah Winfrey introduced made that difficult.

"Our next finalist is Lillian Gilmartin from Boston," Oprah said. "Lillian is already an advice columnist. She writes the very popular 'Luv, Lilly,' column for the *Boston Times.* She is a former newspaper reporter and a former member of the Boston School Committee. Would you welcome her, please."

Lillian, wearing her usual sixteen pounds of jewelry, had fussed with her hair and makeup right up to air time. Now she stared right into the camera. I watched her on the overhead monitor as she waved her fat fingers and batted her overly mascaraed eyelashes at all of America.

Having two finalists from Massachusetts had set the local media in a frenzy. The fact that I was the new face, and male, had made me the man of the hour around Boston. And I liked all the attention. Despite the hectic schedule I felt better than I had in months. Could a man really write an advice column? they wondered. Like the national press, they seemed especially fascinated by the fact that the final seven included Molly's closest friend—and her professional enemy. I was especially fascinated by the fact that Lillian was in the contest at all. There was something suspect about it. Sure, it was hard to imagine Lillian Gilmartin hiding in the bushes of Plum Island with a hunting rifle. But in other ways, Lillian made sense. Certainly, despite her denials, she might have held a long festering hatred for Molly, and she could have flipped out one night and might have run Molly over. Maybe Lillian had a few loose bricks in her chimney.

Finally Oprah came to me. "Our next contestant, also from Massachusetts, is Jeff Scotland. Jeff is a freelance writer and the author of several true crime books. In addition, Jeff worked for three years as a Licensed Independent Clinical Social Worker in private practice in Albuquerque, New Mexico. There he specialized in personal and family counseling. And he is a member of the American Association for Marriage and Family Therapy."

While the audience applauded, as they had for the others, I watched my life pass before my eyes. Certainly the switchboard was lighting up with calls from New Mexicans saying, "That guy is a fake. He was no independent social worker, I never heard of him." And at the Association for Marriage and Family Therapy, no doubt, somebody was scanning through a data bank, saying, "Scotland, Scotland, I don't recall that we have any member by the name of Scotland." And what about that American Association for Marriage, etc., I thought. Shouldn't I have some sort of membership card in my wallet? The fear of being discovered was so unnerving that I sometimes forgot that my mission was to find Molly's murderer. On what show would I be humiliated in front of millions? I wondered. Would it be here, today, on *Oprah*? It was like knowing that someone with a sharp blade was waiting for me in one of the hotel rooms on the tour. What's worse, it appeared that I had lied for nothing. Only the Reverend Cheetham and the lady from Illinois had any counseling background. I prayed that Crash Galovitch wouldn't book us on an Albuquerque TV show.

Oprah went on to introduce Schlagel, the gynecologist, who was the only black person among the finalists, and Noelle Winter, the last finalist.

Noelle, a newspaper reporter from Minneapolis, was my favorite. She was pretty, bright, and sophisticated. She had long brown hair and flashing impish eyes. Noelle and I had become friends immediately and had tried to make each other laugh on a local Cleveland TV show. Between Noelle and me, among all of us really, there was a bond and little sense that we were competing with each other. After all, we had each done something that eighteen thousand other people had failed to do, and now we were all looking out at the world from the same goldfish bowl.

The *Oprah* show went well. We took turns telling the world why we thought we should be the next Molly Collins. Oprah dwelled on the fact that Molly and I were friends, but I got through it okay. Then we took questions from the audience. One woman asked me what she should say to her fifteen-year-old daughter who she thought was being sexually active, and a buzz went through the audience when I told her to get the kid some condoms. The woman didn't care for my solution, but I said it was better than having an unwanted grandchild sleeping on the spare cot for the next twenty years, and it was a hell of a lot better than going to a funeral.

After the audience questions, Oprah threw out a few of her own, for all of us to answer, and we were done. With seven guests on a show, no one gets to say a whole lot. Just as well, I thought. If I were alone, there would have been too much time to discuss my family counseling in Albuquerque.

After the show the others went back to the Hilton Towers, and Noelle and I climbed into a limousine with Crash Galovitch. We were taken to a local network affiliate station, where we taped a five-minute segment for a magazine show that would air that night. The hostess of the show looked to be about twelve, but the show went fine.

Crash seemed nervous throughout. That made sense. After all, he was trying to keep seven finalists and dozens of producers around the country happy, informed, and on schedule. But on the way back to the hotel, Crash sat in front with the driver and said little. I wondered about him. There had been times since I was selected, and even before, when Molly was far from my mind, when I had gotten caught up in the contest itself, seduced by fantasies of winning it and solving all my other problems. But there were other times, and this was one of them, when I obsessed about Molly's murder, when all my theories were like a tape cassette that had been shoved into my brain and played over and over. Yes, I thought now as the limousine wove its way through the downtown streets of Chicago, maybe Lillian Gilmartin had nothing to do with Molly's death, and maybe Crash Galovitch did. After all, it was Crash who had called in November and asked me to stop snooping around. It was Crash who said there could be "benefits" from keeping my mouth shut. It was Crash who was up to his nose in debt to the loan sharks. Maybe Crash had some angle on killing Molly that would help him with his eighty-thousand-dollar problem.

Of course, I thought, it was also possible that Molly was killed by a spurned lover, or an insane fan, or someone who had gotten really rotten advice from her. Or maybe Lillian Gilmartin hired Crash to kill Molly for eighty thousand dollars. Yes, Scotty, I thought, and maybe there was another gunman on the grassy knoll in Dallas.

That evening Noelle and I had dinner at Machine Gun Krepla, a Jewish delicatessen on State Street, where the waiters dress like 1920s gangsters. We sat at a small table in the back and ate corned beef on pumpernickel bread, and kosher pickles, and potato pancakes with applesauce.

Noelle was fascinated by the fact that I knew Molly. She wanted to know everything about her.

"You're not going to crush my illusions and tell me that Molly was really some wretched woman who poisoned pigeons in the park and played loud rap music late at night, are you?"

"No," I said. "Molly loved pigeons, and cats, and Boston, and Beatles music . . ." I stopped. "Jesus," I said, "I sound like Erich Segal."

I told Noelle all my Molly stories, and it came back to me how truly close Molly and I had been.

"Well, it's obvious that you loved her," Noelle said. "Did you ever sleep with her?"

"No," I said.

"Then who do you sleep with?"

"Who do I sleep with?" I said. "What ever happened to 'Where did you grow up?' and 'What college did you go to?'"

Noelle smiled devilishly. "I'm a reporter," she said. "I like to get right to the hard questions."

"I see. You mean, am I married or do I have a girlfriend?"

"Yes."

"I'm legally married," I said. "But my wife bailed out in October. Something about me being a spineless loser who would never amount to twelve cents. As for a girlfriend, yes. No. I don't know."

"It sounds complicated," Noelle said.

"Her name's Joan. She's married. She was Molly's secretary."

Noelle leaned over and beckoned me close with her hand. "Listen," she whispered, "it's important that you give me every sordid detail. I love gossip." Then she leaned back and smiled and said, "Do you love her?"

"Yes," I said. It was the first time I had said it out loud.

"Then it is complicated," Noelle said. "She must have been very jealous of Molly."

"I guess," I said. "I never thought of it that way."

By this time Joan and I had settled into a comfortable routine, which I now described to Noelle. Once a week Joan and I would have dinner and a movie if we could get away with it. And once a week we would meet at a motel and read newspapers and make love.

"It works," I said. "But sometimes I get the feeling

that Joan wants to tell her husband about us just to bring things to a boil."

"Maybe he already knows," Noelle said. "And just doesn't know what to do about it."

"I know that what I'm doing is wrong," I said.

"Stringing Joan along," Noelle said, before I could say it.

"Right."

"And you know you should end it," she added quickly.

"Right, but—"

"But everybody needs somebody," she said.

"Yes," I said. For a moment I wasn't sure whether we were talking about me or Noelle.

After the pickles and pumpernickel, Noelle and I ordered cream soda and cheesecake. It sounds disgusting, but it's what you must do if you're going to do deli right. When we were done, the pistol-packing waiter cleared the table. We ordered coffee. I think neither of us wanted the moment to end.

Noelle stared off for a moment, as if rehearsing some lines in her mind. Then she put her hand on mine.

"Look, Scotty," she said. "I don't want this to come out the wrong way. But I would be less than honest if I didn't tell you that I find you to be a very attractive man."

I actually blushed.

"Does that surprise you?" she asked.

"Some," I said. "I haven't felt very attractive for a while."

Over coffee we talked about Noelle. She had grown up in Duluth, in apartments. Her father repaired watches. Noelle had been a social butterfly until her father died, when she was a teenager, then she went into a shell from which she didn't emerge until she was twenty-five. "I was an introvert for ten years," she said, "from butterfly to caterpillar." Then journalism school, six years at the newspaper in Minneapolis, and now, the contest. There was a short-lived marriage squeezed in there and a couple of romances with older men. "No doubt a father fixation of some sort," she joked.

Then I told Noelle about Mungus and the bowling alley lady, about the funky little cottages on Plum Island, about how good I felt when I was able to give people helpful advice. But I didn't tell her about the murder, or the shooting at the cottage, or even about the time that Fred McHale sliced my throat open like a cantaloupe.

"Plum Island and Minneapolis sound like two different worlds," she said, "but there is one thing we have in common."

"What's that?"

"I'm having an affair with a married man," she said.

"Do you love him?" I asked. We laughed. "Now I sound like an advice columnist," I said.

"Yes," she said. "But I think it's time to move on with my life." Then she said, "I'm thinking of dropping out of the contest."

"Why would you?" I asked. "If you won, that would really be moving on with your life."

"It's hard to explain," she said. "Let's change the subject. Tell me about your wife."

"We loved each other. We stopped loving each other. She left."

From Machine Gun Krepla we walked back to the hotel. It was early March and the weather had gotten mild. Noelle and I walked slowly, close together, but not quite touching.

"March came in like a zebra this year," Noelle said.

"Yes, but I think it will go out like a water buffalo," I replied.

And we kept walking. We didn't laugh. We didn't explain our jokes. We didn't need to.

When we got into the lobby of the Hilton, Noelle invited me up to her room to watch the television show that we had taped that afternoon. In her room, while we waited for the show to come on, we played a game of Scrabble, which Noelle had borrowed from the front desk. Noelle insisted that there was such a word as *scrank,* and also *thurt.* So I let her win.

We ordered popcorn from room service and watched the show. I liked myself on TV. I looked confident. I liked Noelle, too. She looked as if she belonged there.

When it was time for me to leave, I stood by the door.

"Look," I said, "I don't know what's gotten into me. I used to cheat on my wife once in a while, but I don't think I could ever cheat on the woman who's cheating on her husband to be with me. It must be love."

"I understand," Noelle said.

"I've got to straighten that out. But, what I'm trying to say is that, well, if I weren't in love with Joan and you weren't in love with someone . . ."

"I know what you mean," Noelle said. "I feel the same way." She kissed her fingers, then pressed them to my cheek.

The conversation was getting a bit heavy, so I tried to lighten it up on the way out.

"If I don't win, I hope you do," I said. "You look great on television."

She smiled. "Thanks," she said. "But I don't care for all those lights. In that studio I was getting hot enough to burn a wet mule."

"Hot enough to burn a wet mule?" I said. "That's cute. "Doesn't sound like something they'd say in Minnesota."

"Tennessee," she said.

For a lot of reasons I didn't sleep well that night.

CHAPTER 16

"Your wife called," Mungus said.

"My wife?" I said.

"Anne," he said. "You remember her."

We were on Route 1 in North Miami, Florida, riding along in a brand-new silver Ford Taurus, just as if we owned it. Actually, it belonged to Hertz. But the *Patriot* was paying for the rental.

I was in Miami because Crash Galovitch had booked me and the other finalists onto south Florida TV and radio shows. Mungus was in Miami because I had called him from Chicago and asked him if he wanted to meet me in Miami. I figured he was entitled to some of the glamour. "Miami," he had said, "that's the place with the sunshine and the beaches and the beautiful women in bikinis? Yeah, I think I could work that into my schedule." So he had flown in and I had picked him up that morning at Miami airport.

"What did Anne want?" I asked now.

"Who knows?" Mungus said. "She saw you on the *Oprah* show. She sends her congratulations."

"Great," I said.

We were on Route 1 driving north because I had decided to confront Crash Galovitch with my belief that the Molly contest was rigged for Noelle Winter to win. It was an idea I had kept to myself from Chicago to Detroit to Dallas. But it was getting heavier in my mind each day, and I wanted to find out if Crash knew anything about it. I'd looked for Galovitch that morning in the hotel, and the Reverend Cheetham had told me that Crash had gone up to Hollywood. I figured Crash would be at the Hollywood Dog Track.

Mungus and I rarely play the dogs. We prefer to lose our money on poorly chosen horses and the crap tables in Atlantic City. But Crash Galovitch was a guy who craved action, and if the horses had the day off, the dogs would do just fine.

"The phone hasn't stopped ringing," Mungus said as I guided the Taurus slowly through the eternally grid-locked traffic of Dade County. "I've been as busy as a beaver with his head cut off. Everybody wants to know if you're going to be the new 'Dear Molly.' It's not just reporters and friends."

"It's not?"

"It's friends of friends. It's guys who sat beside you on a bus when you were twelve years old. It's women who once borrowed a tampon from your sister. It's 'This Is Your Life, Jeff Scotland.' I expect Ralph Edwards to jump out from behind a curtain with some old crow. 'Yes, Ralph, I knew Scotty when he was in kindergarten. He used to vomit his milk over all the other kids. Yes, he was an adorable little tyke.'"

"Thanks for taking the calls," I said. "Sorry if they're interfering with business."

"Are you kidding? This has been great for business," Mungus said. "People stop in to get advice from you, and

I sell them a T-shirt. This thing is really going to happen,
I can feel it. You really are going to be rich and famous.
Hell, you're already famous."

"Mungus," I said, "don't you get it?" I had already told
him about Noelle's "hot enough to burn a wet mule"
remark.

"Get what?"

"Noelle Winter must be Dracut's girlfriend."

"Of course I get it," Mungus said. "That's the beauty
of it. Instead of a six-to-one shot, you've got a lock on
the job. You're the only one who's got the scam figured
out. Dracut won't go through with it, knowing you can
expose him. Instead, he'll give you the job as a reward
for keeping your mouth shut."

"And what about Molly?" I said.

"What about her?"

"She was murdered, damn it. I'm supposed to be
figuring out who did it, right? Well Lawrence Dracut is
looking like a hell of a good suspect right about now. Do
you seriously think I'd work for a guy who murdered my
best friend? How goddamned low do you think I've
sunk?"

"Of course I don't think you would," Mungus said,
seriously. "All I'm saying is that if Dracut had nothing to
do with Molly's death, then I think you should take the
job."

"And if Dracut did kill Molly?"

"Then we hire Lorena Bobbitt to do some surgery on
him."

By the time we pulled into the entrance for the
Hollywood Dog Track, the dogs had been running for an
hour, and the parking lot was packed. We parked the
Taurus near the entrance and walked past the long rows
of cars, across the parking lot, to the clubhouse. Along

the way we passed a lot of early losers who were on their way out. They were mostly old guys with cigar butts jammed between their teeth, all of them staring intently at the program list of the next day's entries and planning their comeback. Is this how Mungus and I are going to end up? I wondered.

"You think Galovitch knows it's fixed?" Mungus said as we made our way through the clubhouse turnstile. "Why would he urge you to get in?"

"Because I was Molly's friend," I said. "Having me as a contestant is like having Molly's seal of approval on the contest. Joan figured that out a long time ago."

"Sharp lady," Mungus said.

We found Crash Galovitch on the second level of the clubhouse, hunched like a bookkeeper over his lists and charts. He sat at a table by the window, above the gate for the 5/16th-mile races.

"Hey, Scotty," he called when he saw me, "I didn't know you played the dogs."

"I don't," I said. I introduced Mungus. "I'm just here looking for you."

"Great," Crash said. "One second, while I write this down." He squinted into the sunlight as he tried to make out the numbers on the toteboard. "Twenty-one bucks on the quinella," he said. "I was hoping for more, but hey, it's better than a kick in the rear end, huh?"

Mungus and I sat down while Crash went to collect his money and place a bet for the next race. We could hear the greyhounds yelping in their stalls.

"You guys want a drink?" Crash said when he came back. Without waiting for an answer he signaled the waitress.

"Everything okay?" he said. "You like your room? Food okay? Get yourself some room service, sit by the pool, check out the snatch. Enjoy it. We got no gigs until tonight's reception."

"The room's fine," I said. "That's not what I want to talk about."

"You want some girls? I got friends down here, I'll get you some girls."

"We don't need any girls," I said.

"Well, actually we do," Mungus put in. "We're all out of them."

"Look, Crash, we've got to talk," I said.

"Wait a minute," Crash said. He glanced up at one of the television monitors. "It's post time."

"Jesus, Crash," I said, "this is important."

By this time "Lucky" the mechanical bunny was making his way around the track, and Crash was mesmerized. Mungus leaned over and whispered in my ear, "Tell him yes, we do need some girls."

The dogs went off, and Crash held his fist to his mouth while his dog, a fifty-nine-pound speed demon named Nuts in an Uproar came out in the lead. "That's the way, girl, that's the way," Crash kept saying. "Keep your foot to the metal, keep it up, keep it up."

Nuts in an Uproar led the field into the backstretch, then fell back as if she'd been lassoed from behind.

"Friggin' beast died on me," Crash said a few seconds later when it was over, and his dog had finished last. "They say you can't bribe a dog, but I'm telling you, that mutt took a dive."

Crash wanted to go back to his racing form and pick a winner in the next race, but I was in no mood to be ignored.

"What the hell's going on, Crash?" I said. "Is the contest fixed?"

"Fixed?" he said. His pencil fell to the table. Suddenly his racing form was forgotten.

"Noelle Winter," I said. "I think she's Dracut's girl-friend."

Crash looked shocked. He sat down. "Why?"

"Something she said," I told him. "I know she's having an affair with a married man. I know she likes older men. She probably met Dracut at one of those newspaper conferences."

"Jesus," Crash said.

"So? Is it fixed?"

"Scotty, I swear, this is the first time I heard about this. It makes sense now that you say it. Dracut asked me to keep an eye on her on the road, but he said it was because he didn't want any sex scandals, you know, potential Mollys fucking each other. He figured Noelle was the only one the guys would be after. That's what he said, I swear."

Crash glanced at the screen where the odds were displayed for the next race. But he seemed, for once, not to be into the race. He seemed stunned.

"Shit," he said. "Let me think for a minute." He stared down at the table, then up at me, then down at the table. "Shit," he said again. And then, "I've got it. Look, you call Dracut."

"Me?"

"Right. You tell him you know what he's up to, and you're going to blow the whole thing if he doesn't give you the job. He would do anything not to have his wife know."

"Blackmail?" I said.

"Well, why not?" Crash said. "If he rigged this contest, then he's screwing you and all the others, isn't he?"

"I don't know," I said.

"Do it, Scotty, this is your big break. I'll back you up. I've been telling Dracut all along that you're the best person for the job."

Mungus and I didn't stay long, just long enough for Crash to urge me again and again to confront Dracut. I never told him I would. I never told him I wouldn't. It didn't seem to trouble him that we would be screwing all the other finalists.

On the way out Mungus asked me, "How come you didn't tell Crash to go fuck himself? You know damn well you're not going to blackmail Lawrence Dracut."

"Because I don't trust Crash Galovitch."

"I thought he was your friend," Mungus said.

"No," I said. "You're my friend. Crash is just a guy I used to be in business with."

"So you're saying he's a slime," Mungus said.

"I guess," I said.

"You're probably right," Mungus said. "But I tell you, I'd like him a lot better if he sent a couple of girls to our room."

When we got back to the hotel that afternoon, I called Lillian Gilmartin in her room. Despite the new developments, I hadn't been able to put it completely out of my mind that Lillian had a reason to kill Molly and was possibly nuts enough to do it. I thought that if I confronted her I could get the truth.

"Scotty!" she said when I called. She sounded pleased to hear from me.

"I was wondering if we could have a talk," I said.

"Well, sure. You want to meet me in the lounge?"

"How about if I come to your room?" I said.

"Oh," she said. "I understand. Yes, that would be just fine. Why don't you give me a little time, though."

"Half an hour?"

"Fine," she said.

A half hour later Lillian greeted me at the door. She wore an embarrassingly feminine blue peignoir and stunk of too much perfume.

"Come in," she said. "I'm so glad we have this chance to talk." She swept across the room and deposited her large body on a delicate pink love seat. She had pulled the drapes. Only a single lamp by the bed lighted the room. Soft romantic music played on the radio. Ice and soft drinks, along with two glasses, had been neatly set on a tray on the dresser. I sat on the bed.

We talked for a moment about the contest. "Quite the thing, isn't it," she said. "I wonder what the nitwit sisters think of all this." She made a sour smile. "Scotty," she said, smiling demurely as she lifted one massive leg and crossed it over the other, "I want you to know that if I don't win this contest, I hope you do." Her plum cheeks rose. "I think it would be refreshing to have a man in the field." She glanced me up and down. "Especially one as cute as you," she said. "So if you win I want you to know there's no hard feelings. Would you like a drink?"

She moved to the dresser and poured us each a cola. She handed me a glass. "Wish I had some munchies to serve you," she said, "but we'll have to make do." She lifted her glass toward me. "Cheers, as they say." She sat again on the love seat.

"Actually," I said slowly, "I'm also hoping that you win if I don't."

"Really?" she seemed pleased. She shifted slightly and the hem of the peignoir rose slightly to reveal the thick pink flesh of her calves. When I am seventy, I wondered, will I desire something like this?

"Yes," I said. "Things have not been going well for me in recent months and I'm going to need the money."

I felt like a skunk, doing this, but I had to know.

"Money, you say?"

"Lillian, I'll get to the point. I know you killed Molly Collins."

Lillian stared at me somewhat fiercely. She took deep breaths and her breasts rose like waves beneath the delicate satin of her nightgown. Then she laughed nervously.

"But, Scotty, I thought you got over that foolishness a long time ago. Me kill Molly? That's absurd."

"I don't think so," I said.

Lillian stood up slowly, patted down her garments in ladylike fashion. Then she walked to the dresser and picked up the tray with the drinks on it, and flung it wildly across the room. The bottle of soda bounced off the wall and one of the glasses shattered.

"You have some nerve!" Lillian roared. Now her eyes were totally wild and she seemed larger than before, dangerously large. "You have some nerve. I thought you would come here and I would show you a good time. Instead . . ." She thrust her arm out, its flab fluttering like a flag in the wind. *"This!"* she shouted. "I don't know what you're trying to pull. But it's not going to work. You've got to get up pretty early in the morning to get the better of Lilly Gilmartin."

Her face was red.

"Jesus!" she shouted, now pacing across the room. Her slippered feet landed like hooves on the deep green carpet. "I can't believe you would do this to me."

I let her rave for a while. She moved back and forth across the room like a horse trying to buck a rider.

"I'm sorry," I said.

"What?" She looked at me suddenly, as if she'd forgotten I was there.

"I'm sorry. It's just that I had to know. Molly was my friend."

"Oh, dear," she said, so softly that it seemed as if another person had entered her body. "You are troubled by this, aren't you." She came over to where I sat. All the red was drained from her body, all the fire extinguished as suddenly as it had been ignited.

"I apologize," I said. I wanted to keep her calm. I was unnerved by how quickly her mood had changed.

I held my head down in a posture of regret. I felt her hand gently on my neck. God, I thought, I hope she doesn't want to hop in bed with me after all this.

"Molly was my friend," I said again. I sat there for a long time pretending to be grief-stricken.

"I forgive you, dear," Lillian said. Her hand began massaging my neck. "I suppose it's understandable. Everyone thinks I hated Molly. But I didn't, I really didn't."

She pressed close to me, and I could feel one of her massive breasts against my face. It smelled like the cosmetics counter at Filene's. Soon her fingers worked their way down to my chest. "Let's just forget this ever happened," Lillian said. "Forgive and forget, that's what I always say." She undid the top button on my shirt. Am I to be punished for this stunt? I wondered.

"God, it gets so lonely on these road trips, doesn't it," she said, as if we were the Red Sox and did this all the time. Her fingers played with the hair on my chest. "Poor, poor baby," she said.

Cautiously I pushed her hand away. "Not now," I said. "I'm too emotional." Would there be another explosion?

I wondered. I gave her a smile. "Perhaps we could get together later."

Her eyes shone like a smitten young girl's. "Yes," she said. "That would be lovely."

At the door she kissed me on the lips. It was a horror I could not prevent. I didn't want to set her off again.

As I returned to my room I thought about Lillian's outburst. I didn't know if it proved that she was innocent or proved that she was insane, or both.

That evening at the hotel there was a reception and dinner for the final seven. I arrived a bit late because I'd gone to some effort to call Joan. I wanted to tell her that I was thinking about her, that I missed her. But no one answered her phone.

At least a dozen reporters showed up for the reception. With the exception of the original Mercury astronauts, we had become the most famous group of seven since Snow White. Even Mungus dressed for the occasion, though under his jacket he did wear a T-shirt that said I'M SCHIZOPHRENIC AND SO AM I.

The reception was held in a small meeting room on the hotel mezzanine. We all politely drank cocktails and mingled with the press and posed for pictures and talked into microphones. I had an urge to tell my secret. "Hey everybody!" I wanted to shout. "Lawrence Dracut is shtupping one of the contestants, the whole thing is fixed," but that would have been impolite, so I held my tongue and drank instead. The drinks were free and I'd been feeling healthier lately, so I didn't count the cocktails, I just drank them.

Mungus circulated, too. He told reporters he was an ex-National Hockey League player, defenseman with the

Pittsburgh Penguins. But mostly he lobbied for me with the press, especially the ones who wore skirts.

"Scotty once saved my life in a rooming house fire," I heard him tell one reporter. And he told another that I had captured Fred McHale, which I guess is true, if reporting a dead body while bleeding profusely from the neck can be considered a capture.

After cocktails we dined in a suite overlooking Biscayne Bay. Before the seating, Crash Galovitch and I stared down at the multimillion-dollar yachts in the bay and reminisced about the days when he lived on a boat not far from where we were, and some of his clients that I wrote stories about.

There were thirteen of us at dinner. Crash had selected a few reporters to dine with us. Lawrence Dracut's wife, an affable woman with a radiant smile, had flown down to act as hostess for the event. Dracut, we were told, had been detained on business. We sat at a long and elegant table, and, as it happened, I ended up sitting, uncomfortably, next to Noelle.

Ever since Noelle's "wet mule" remark I had been cool with her. The remark had led me quickly to the conclusion that she was a secret girlfriend of Lawrence Dracut, and that the "Dear Molly" contest was designed to get her a great job at the *Patriot*, where Dracut could get to her without a "business trip." I had not been able to get it out of my mind that, by letting Dracut rig the contest in her favor, Noelle was stealing from me and the other finalists. Of course, it also occurred to me that I was attempting to do the same thing when I invented my Albuquerque counseling credits, but it was easy to rationalize that away with the knowledge that if I won, it would be on my advice-giving skills, and if Noelle won, it would be on her bedroom skills. It was not a gallant thought, but I wasn't feeling very gallant. As one of the finalists I felt betrayed, and as just plain Scotty I was jealous. I could have written a great advice letter to a guy like me. "Tell her you're pissed at her," I would say. But if I had learned one thing from Molly, it was that being a great advice-giver didn't necessarily mean that you always did the mature thing in your own life. So I bit my lip and made chitchat with Noelle.

"Scotty, is something wrong?" she asked.

"No," I said. "Why?"

"I don't know. It just seems as if lately you act as if you borrowed money from me and haven't paid it back."

"Just tired," I said, and she let it die.

In time Noelle gave up on me and worked to her left, where Jill Levinson sat. Jill, enthusiastically unaware of the fact that she had no chance of becoming the next Molly Collins, chatted amicably with the woman who was defrauding her. It annoyed the hell out of me that I still liked Noelle.

After dinner the press went home and most of the finalists gathered in the hotel's "Sweet Seventies" lounge, a dark and heavily air-conditioned room, decorated with huge posters of convicted Watergate figures, headlines from the 1970s, and one of those mechanical bulls which were popular for about ten minutes back in the late 1970s. We jammed a couple of tables together and gathered around them. The lounge was fairly quiet. Soft music came from somewhere, and only one couple danced on the small parquet floor. I prayed that Noelle would not ask me to dance with her.

I had swallowed two glasses of wine during the reception and more at dinner. Now I ordered another drink. Mungus, who had also had a few, began reading imaginary letters to the group.

"Dear So-and-So," he said, placing his empty hands in front of him as if he held a letter, "I think my marriage is in trouble. My wife goes out every night, and two or three times a week she comes home with strange men. She says they are her cousins, but several of them have been members of different races. Also, she asks me odd questions, like what size shirt would I wear if I were six inches taller. I don't want to come right out and accuse her of cheating on me, but I feel I have a right to know. And it's signed . . ." Mungus thought it over. "Jealous in Joliet," he said.

Everybody raised a glass and cheered while Mungus thought of his answer.

"Dear Jealous," he answered, "It's obvious that you are trying to ruin your marriage. Don't you know that a lifelong relationship is based on trust? Straighten up, pal, or get some counseling."

Mungus put down his imaginary letter and picked up another one. I ordered another drink.

"Dear So-and-So," Mungus said, "My sister and I disagree. She says there is no God and never has been, and that life is devoid of meaning. She says the universe is just a pointless accident and we're all doomed to eternal oblivion. Is she right? It's signed 'Doomed in Dallas.'"

Mungus smiled and came up with something right away.

"Dear Doomed," he said, "I had a sister like that once. It was a great relief to all of us when she killed herself."

Everybody laughed, and Mungus started another letter. It went on like that. Soon all of us were making up letters and giving dreadful advice. Noelle was exhausted, and she took an early leave. As she passed by me on her way out, she touched my shoulder, then she looked into my

face and tried to solve the mystery of my behavior.
"Maybe tomorrow we'll get a chance to talk," she said.

"Maybe," I said.

By midnight only Lillian, Ted Schlagel, and Jean
Stone were left to carouse with me. There were a few
other people in the lounge, but it had been a slow night
and now the dance floor was empty. The place was
beginning to smell like the bottom of a beer bottle.
Mungus had run out of material, and now he stood at the
bar, telling some woman that he and Wayne Gretzky
were half brothers.

Ted Schlagel had turned out to be a pretty decent
fellow, and I felt sorry for him because he hated
gynecology and saw this Molly job as his ticket out. He
wasn't afraid to admit that he wanted to win the job more
than he had ever wanted anything. He thought he could
be a real role model for black kids.

"I don't think you should plan on getting the job," I
said, somewhat bitterly and somewhat drunkenly. By this
time I had gotten to the bottom of several glasses of
wine.

"Because?" Ted said sharply. He had taken my comment as criticism.

"Think about it," I said. "Do you believe they're going
to give this job to a stranger, someone who can turn
around in a year and say, 'Thanks for making me the new
Molly Collins, I guess I'll go it alone now?'" I was
trying hard to plagiarize what Hattie Slater had said to
me, but I was slurring my words. "No," I went on.
"They're going to pick Dracut's wife's hairdresser or
maybe the guy who sells him steel-belted radial tires. Or
maybe they have a dog."

"A dog?" Ted said.

"Yeah, a dog," I said. The dog thing made some kind of twisted sense to me in my soused state. "Maybe someone who shampoos their dog is very good at giving advice, or—"

"You're drunk," Ted said.

"The gardener," I said. "Yeah, that's it, a gardener will be the next Molly Collins."

"Boy, you're really drunk," Ted said. Now he was laughing.

"It's irrelevant," I said nonsensically. I slumped in my chair and stared at my wineglass. Then I pulled myself up dramatically and looked at Lillian, then Jean, then Ted.

"A very wise woman named Hattie Slater once said, and I quote, 'It's in the bag.'"

"You're saying the thing is fixed?" Jean asked.

"Can you keep a secret?" I said. I held my wineglass high in my unsteady hand and watched the wine in it wiggle as if I were sitting on a moving train.

Ted nodded. I looked at Lillian. She nodded. I looked at Jean Stone. She nodded. I knew, even in my cloud of alcohol, that they were humoring me, but as they leaned closer there was an expectancy, as if they thought I might tell them something that they had suspected all along.

"Dracut," I said, "is fucking one of the finalists. I'll give you a hint." Then I let out with an explosive "MOO" that echoed across the dark lounge and startled the few remaining customers.

"Moo?" Lillian said.

"Yes, Moo," I said. "Minnesota. Aren't there a lot of cows in Minnesota?"

"Minnesota?" Jean said.

"Noelle Winter," Ted explained. "Scotty, are you

saying that Lawrence Dracut is sleeping with Noelle Winter?"

"Does the pope shit in the woods?" I said.

"And he knew her before the contest began?"

I looked him straight in the eye.

"Moo," I said.

The last thing I remember before passing out was that Ted seemed very angry. I heard him say, "We'd better all talk about this in the morning." And I remember Lillian leaning over me and touching me. She was surprisingly gentle. "Why don't you go to bed," she said. "You've had a lot to drink."

It was Mungus who got me to my feet and took me up to our bedroom. "Ohio," he said as he put me on my bed and placed some covers over me. "The woman gave me her phone number in Ohio. In case I'm coming through sometime. Scotty, what sort of person would be coming through Ohio sometime?"

I was awakened at five o'clock that morning by the high-pitched shriek of the hotel's fire alarm. I glanced at Mungus's bed. He was not there. Probably went back to spend the night with his Ohio lady, I figured. I've been in at least a dozen hotels where the fire alarms went off at night and there was never a fire, so I wasn't concerned. If I had been in town alone, I would have stayed in bed. But I knew that if I didn't show up in the lobby, the others would come looking for me. Besides, what if there really was a fire? So I climbed out of bed and started to look for clothes before I realized I was already dressed.

The corridor wasn't exactly mobbed with hysterical guests. Six or eight were waiting for the elevator, even though there were signs that said don't use the elevators in the event of a fire. These were the cautious few who were even bothering to get out of bed. They had, apparently, been through as many false alarms as I had, and unless they saw flames licking at their bedroom door, they weren't going to believe there really was a fire, and they sure as hell weren't going to walk down twenty-three flights of stairs.

When I got to the lobby, there were maybe a hundred people there. Clearly, most of the guests had chosen to ignore the alarm. Many of my fellow finalists were there, and it occurred to me that none of them had pounded on my door on the way down. Perhaps we were more competitive than I thought. The night manager was explaining that so far they hadn't found a fire, but we should stay put until they were sure.

"Someone set off an alarm on the twenty-third floor," he said.

"The twenty-third!" I said. That was our floor.

"Yes, but there's nothing to be concerned about."

Now there was another alarm, this one inside me, and it was urgently shrieking that Noelle was in danger.

"Where's Noelle?" I said. Nobody had seen her.

I bolted for the elevator. When it came I pushed my way in, jabbing two or three people who were getting off. I pushed at the button for the twenty-third floor. I pushed it again and again, as if that would make it work faster. "Come on, goddamnit!" I screamed. The people in the lobby stared at me. Finally the doors closed and the elevator began its agonizingly slow rise.

I paced back and forth in the small cage. My heart was beating furiously. Either this alarm was a ruse of some sort, or I was being dangerously paranoid. At last the elevator stopped at twenty-three, and I jumped out and ran as fast as I could down the long corridor to Noelle's room. I was disgracefully out of shape, and just this short sprint made me breathless. When I got to Noelle's door, I rapped hard. Even in my desperation and fear I thought, Jesus, I'm going to make a fool of myself. "Noelle," I called. "Are you all right?" No answer. I just had to know that she was okay. I hit the door harder. This time it moved. The door was open. As I pushed it away from me and stepped inside, there was a moment of absolute certainty that I would find Noelle lifeless on the bed, her throat slit by some McHale-like creature.

The lamp next to Noelle's bed was on. The bed was empty. The covers had been thrown off carelessly, as if she had been called out while sleeping. The clothes she had worn earlier were draped over a chair. I looked in the bathroom to be sure. No, she was gone. She had left the room. Thank God, I thought.

But suddenly I thought of Molly, of her being hit by a car. And, with a sickening jolt of fear, I thought, of course Noelle wouldn't be murdered in her bed. This is a person who makes things look like accidents.

Think Scotty, think, I told myself. The stairs, I thought, the twenty-three flights of stairs. I dashed out of the room and ran down the long corridor the other way, past the elevators, past the few people who were straggling back to their rooms. My feet pounded like pistons on the long floral carpet. The doors seemed to whiz past me, as if I were standing still and the hotel was moving. At the end of the corridor I came to the thick metal fire door. I pushed it open. The air that was trapped in the stairwell was stale and salty from the ocean breezes. The stairs were gray and harsh-looking. In the dim yellow light they had an unfinished look, as if the building were still being constructed. An orange metal rail guarded the left side of the stairwell. As I peered down over the railing, I could see straight down for twenty-three stories. It was a dizzying pit that led to an unforgiving gray stone floor. Even from that distance I knew that the twisted figure at the bottom, that looked like a broken doll, was Noelle. And long before I got to her, I knew that she was dead.

CHAPTER 17

Lawrence Dracut, wearing a silk shirt beneath a suede jacket, was waiting for me when I got to Zachary's restaurant at The Colannade hotel on Huntington Avenue. Zachary's was one of seventeen restaurants widely regarded as the best in the city. I was there because Crash Galovitch had called and said that Dracut wanted to meet me for dinner. I had gone because it was a free meal. And because Dracut had been a part of Noelle's life.

When I got to Dracut, he seemed to smile broadly as he rose from a table that was elegantly set with linen and silver. He shook my hand. For a moment he seemed so vigorous and cheerful that I thought, my God, this man has been carved from a block of ice. But the smile dissolved quickly, and when I looked more closely, I saw that Lawrence Dracut was in greater pain than I was. Our eyes met only for a second, but it was like glancing into a cave, and I knew that I was looking at the one place where Dracut could not hide his pain.

"Difficult times," he said somberly.

"Yes," I said.

It had been only a week since Noelle had died. Her

body had been shipped back to Minnesota for burial. The "Dear Molly" publicity tour had been, mercifully, called off. The finalists had gone home to wait for an announcement. Outside of The Colonnade it was a fine spring evening in Boston, the kind that stirs memories of high school romances and schoolyard whiffleball games. It was the kind of sweet spring evening that ordinarily would fill me with a feverish optimism. But I was numb inside. For a week the tough questions had pelted my mind without letup. Had Noelle been tossed to her death because I had shot off my mouth about her being the inevitable winner of the "Dear Molly" job? Or had that tragic fall really been an accident?

A waiter came, and Dracut ordered drinks for both of us. Wine for me, root beer for himself.

"My wife only lets me drink on weekends," he explained.

"Look," I said, "I want you to know that I'm sorry if your wife found out about you and Noelle because of me."

I knew that this wouldn't exactly be a newsflash to Lawrence Dracut. He was the kind of man who found out things, and I figured that by now he had heard about my drunken rambling.

"She didn't," Dracut said.

"I kind of got drunk and shot my mouth off that night in Miami," I said.

"I know," he said.

That night in Miami, I thought. Only seven more sleepless nights had passed since Noelle had smashed into the stone floor at the bottom of the stairwell, but it felt to me as if that tragedy had happened long ago in a dreadful dream, and that dream had become a permanent part of my awareness.

"How did you know about us?" Dracut asked.

"Noelle told me she was having an affair with a married man," I said.

"That's it?"

"An older married man," I explained.

"Oh."

"Then she used one of your Tennessee expressions."

Dracut managed a slight smile. "You still have a lot of detective in you," he said.

"Yes," I said.

"She was . . ." Dracut said. Then he stopped and left his sentence unfinished. For a moment he looked lost. He tugged an antique gold railroad watch from the front pocket of his jacket and stared at it. He wasn't checking to see what time it was. He was just trying to find something to focus on so he wouldn't fall apart. I understood. I'd been running that same play for a week. When he spoke again, it was intimately. He said, "I really loved her, you know. It wasn't just a case of some old fool's sap rising in the presence of female youth."

"I know," I said, though truly I had no idea one way or the other.

"Did you know she could sing?" he asked.

"No," I said.

"Like a songbird," he said. "I'd play my guitar and she would sing. The old tunes. I don't care for anything that's been written since 1952. It was wonderful to hear her. The sex was quite exceptional, of course. But it wasn't the main thing."

He picked up the menu then, I think to hide his face.

"A terrible accident," he said. "Terrible."

I chose not to tell Lawrence Dracut that Noelle might have been murdered. If he was involved, which I doubted, I didn't want him to know I knew. And if he wasn't involved, there was no point in salting his wounds.

"You know what's the hardest part," Dracut said.

It wasn't really a question, but I answered it, anyhow.

"Not being able to share your grief with the person who's dead," I said.

He gave me a look of great respect and said, "Christ, I bet you can see right through me, can't you."

"No. But I lost a friend a while back, too," I said.

"Oh, yes," he said. "Miss Collins. Sorry." Then "It's also tough having to act cheerful at home. But there are certain things in this world that you cannot share with the woman in your life. And at the top of that list is the fact that you've had another woman in your life. Even if you've lost her. I really loved the heck out of that girl."

When the waiter brought our drinks, Dracut held his glass of root beer high and swirled it gently. He took a long pull on it as if it were a glass of bourbon, and I could see in his face that he must have been one wild-living reprobate in his time. Then he sat up straight in his chair, placed his forearms on the table, and leaned forward.

"Well," he said, "enough whining. I loved her, she's gone, that's it. I don't like whiners. I think we should hang the lot of them." He winked at me. "So I'd better pull myself together before someone slips a noose around my sorry neck. Can't very well bring the girl back by whining about how I've lost her, now can I."

"No," I said. I understood. Dracut had probably ordered himself a thousand times to stop obsessing about Noelle's death, had insisted to himself that there was nothing he could do about it, that it was time to move on. But I knew from my own mournful week that pushing these thoughts from the mind was like constantly lifting heavy weights, and when your strength was sapped, they landed back on you with force and permanence. I knew that Lawrence Dracut would smile his way through dinner like an incumbent congressman, but it would be months, maybe years, before the glint of mischief would again sparkle in his eyes.

"By the way," Dracut said slyly, "how's your profile of me for *Glitz* coming along? You know the one I mean. The one you're writing for my old friend Hattie Slater."

I didn't answer.

Dracut let me dangle on that hook for a while, and then he said, "You know, my keys disappeared the day you interviewed me. For that profile in *Glitz*. And they reappeared the very next day. Strangest damn thing."

He shook his head, as if life were just full of amusing mysteries.

"Do you still believe that Miss Collins was murdered?" he asked.

There was no way for me to tell him yes without explaining that Noelle might also have been murdered by someone who didn't want her selected for the job.

"No," I said, "I don't think she was murdered."

"I see," he said, nodding subtly to acknowledge that I was lying, and that he knew I was lying, and that we both knew that he knew I was lying.

Whatever Lawrence Dracut really wanted to discuss was left undiscussed through dinner, which Dracut was paying for. He ordered the biggest steak they had, and I ordered the most expensive meal on the menu. We talked mostly about news reporting. That is, he talked, I listened. The phrase "pansy journalists," was used often, as was "gullible public," "great unwashed," and "Ivy League loser with his head up his ass."

After dinner Dracut ordered more wine for me and another root beer for himself. There was some nice expensive desserts on the menu, but I passed on them. Dracut relaxed in his chair and looked satisfied.

"That," he said, "was a fine dinner."

"And free," I said. "It's only going to cost you some green pieces of paper."

"Right," he said. He tucked two fingers into his jacket pocket, reaching for a cigar before remembering that he no longer smoked. Then he leaned forward, looked me over carefully, as if he were reconsidering a major purchase, and finally got to the point.

"The reason we are here," he said, "is so that I can offer you a job."

"Covering tragic fires in tenement houses?" I said.

Dracut grinned. He was pleased that I remembered our conversation.

"No," he said. "This job is considerably more remunerative than that. The job is nationally syndicated advice columnist."

"Molly's job?"

"You won it," he said. "The committee voted for you."

"How did you vote?" I asked.

"I voted for you, too," he said. He pushed his hand across the table. "Congratulations."

"I don't want it," I said.

Dracut looked at me as if I'd dropped three aces on the table when he was sure I had two pair.

"What do you mean you don't want it? You won it."

"Not fairly," I said.

"Oh?"

"I lied to get it. In my letter of application I said that I worked as a counselor for two years in Albuquerque. The only time I've been to Albuquerque, I wasn't there long enough to tie my shoe."

"Oh, that," he said. He scooped up his drink again, relieved by the fact that nothing important had been said.

"'Oh, that?'" I asked. "You knew?"

"Well, of course I knew it, boy. You don't think I'm going to turn over a big job like this to anybody without checking him out, do you?"

"But it was a lie," I said. "There was no counseling."

"Scotty," he said, "nobody gives a rat's ass about whether or not you lied in your letter of application. If you can give good advice and do it cleverly, do you think anybody cares whether or not you're a psychiatrist or a Ph.D.? You could be a witch doctor, for all the difference it makes. Do you think Ann Landers or 'Dear Abby' or Molly had any education as therapists?"

"No," I said.

"Of course they didn't," he said.

"But they didn't pretend that they had."

"Son, there are lies that matter and there are lies that don't. This is one that don't."

"It matters to me," I said.

Dracut looked me in the eye. His left hand played with the very expensive-looking gold bracelet that he wore on his right wrist. It was no idle movement. He knew what he was doing.

"Do you have any idea of how much money you are turning down?" he said. The message was clear: you could have nice things, like this bracelet.

"Money's not important," I said. "It's just a way of keeping score."

Dracut liked that, and for a moment I thought he would end the conversation just so that we could end with me quoting him.

"Well, maybe," he said. "But look, your lie doesn't bother me and I pride myself on being an honest man."

"Honest?" I almost laughed in his face.

"To a reasonable degree," he said.

"You rigged the contest so that your girlfriend would win, and you call yourself honest?"

"'I have made mistakes,'" Dracut said. "'But I have never made the mistake of claiming that I never made one.'"

I said nothing.

"James Gordon Bennet," he explained. And then, "Look, Scotty, any man can have a lapse in judgment from time to time. I was in love. When a man is under the spell of a beautiful woman, it is sometimes hard to tell him from a fool."

"Who's that?" I said. "William Shakespeare?"

"No. Just Lawrence Dracut," he said.

I felt sorry for him. I hadn't known Noelle long, but I could imagine how wretched it would feel to love her and then lose her.

"Who gets the job if I don't take it?" I said.

"The Reverend Cheetham," he said. "My wife feels strongly that it should be a man."

"Smart woman," I said. "Call Cheetham. Tell him he won. There's no need to tell him he was second choice. Some lies don't matter."

"That's it?" he said.

"That's it," I said.

When I got back to the cottage, the first thing I heard was Mungus screaming "Dolly Madison, you imbecile." He was watching the late-night syndication of *Jeopardy*. He sat on the living room couch eating barbecued potato chips out of an ice bucket. I was surprised to see him home so soon from his date with the bowling alley woman. "Hey, Scotty, I've got nine thousand dollars," he announced proudly, "and these morons have only got six thousand among the three of them."

"Great," I said somberly.

"He offered you the job, didn't he?" Mungus said.

"Yes."

"And you didn't take it."

"Right."

"I figured," he said.

"I can go upstairs and get my gun," I said. "If you'd like to shoot me."

"No, that's okay," he said. "I didn't really want to be a rich stooge with a red Corvette and lots of beautiful women around all the time, anyhow."

"Sorry," I said. "How was your date?"

"I think we're getting to the end of the line," he said. "She talked a lot tonight about how important it was for a man to earn a good living."

"Women," I said. "Who writes their material?"

After *Jeopardy* ended, Mungus, eleven thousand dollars richer, fell asleep on the couch, and ten minutes later his body went upstairs to bed. Without actually waking up, he remembered on his way up the stairs to tell me, "By the way, your wife called again."

I had never returned Anne's first call. Now it was almost midnight. What the hell did she want? I wondered. I decided to call her and get it over with.

"Anne," I said when she answered.

"Scotty," she said.

"Mungus told me you called," I said.

"Yes. I did."

"I've been traveling," I said.

"I saw you on *Oprah*," Anne said. "You're a pretty famous guy these days."

"Yes," I said. "I thought I was pretty hot stuff, being

on *Oprah*. But I turned her on the next day, and she had 'mothers who think their daughters wear too much makeup.' It kind of brought my hat size down a bit."

Anne didn't laugh. She had never really found me all that amusing.

We both let some silence flow by. Then she said, "So, how have you been?"

"Fine," I said. We sounded like two people who had once shared a long cab ride.

"I've been missing you," she said. And then, when I didn't reply, she said, "Perhaps we could. See each other. And talk."

"No," I said.

"Oh," she said.

I let her hang up first. It seemed like the chivalrous thing to do.

CHAPTER 18

"Are you Mr. Scotland?" the girl asked when I answered the door at the cottage. She was a slim, long-haired Italian-looking teenager who smiled stiffly as if she had come for dentistry.

"Yes."

She looked down and fidgeted with the zipper on her blue denim jacket. "I saw you on television."

Then she glanced up, and gave me a look which I had seen a lot lately. It was the look of a person who wanted advice.

"Come on in," I said. "What's your name?"

"Cindy."

Cindy came in and sat on one of the overstuffed chairs that Mungus had bought for a dollar each at a rummage sale.

"Little Debbies?" I asked.

"Huh?"

"Little Debbies. They're cookies. Would you like some?"

"Sure," she said nervously.

"And hot chocolate?" I said. I figured that's what kids drank, hot chocolate with little marshmallows on top.

"Tea would be fine," she said. And then, "I don't want to bother you. It's just, I don't know who else to talk to, and you seemed nice on television."

I walked into the kitchen and put a teapot of water over one of the gas burners. I grabbed the few Little Debbies that Mungus hadn't devoured, and put them on a plate. So this is what it would be like, I thought. If I'd had a kid, she'd be about Cindy's age now and I'd be making tea and cookies for her and she would be coming to me for advice. Of course, the only difference was that Cindy would probably hang on every word I spoke, because she had seen me on TV, and if I really had a daughter, she would laugh at my advice behind my back and tell her friends that I was an old fool, and she would do exactly as she pleased. Kids, I thought.

I placed the tea and cookies on a lap tray and brought it into the living room. I sat near Cindy in the other cheap chair.

"Is it your boyfriend?" I asked.

Cindy stared at me as if I had pulled a rabbit from a hat.

"How did you know that?" she asked.

"I guessed," I said. I had learned from experience that with girls her age it was always the boyfriend or the mother.

Cindy sipped some tea, ate a cookie with blinding speed, and then she started talking and she didn't come up for air for fifteen minutes. I had found, in my short stint as an advice guru, that when people say they need advice, they mostly just need to talk.

The boyfriend's name was Glenn, a kid just like Cindy. Glenn was eighteen and had a hot temper. They had been going together for two years. Glenn, Cindy said, was sweet and considerate most of the time. He had taken her to a Richard Marx concert even though it cost him his week's paycheck from the Market Basket where he was a cashier. "He's really good at it," she explained. But sometimes when Glenn got frustrated, he would smack Cindy right in the face. She twisted her head to show me a welt under her ear. Cindy would cry, she said. Then they would make up. Glenn would promise never to hit her again. Then he would smack her again. She would cry. They would make up again. Again and again they would go through this two-act play, like an alcoholic and his co-dependent wife. What, Cindy asked, should she do?

By this time I had drained my teacup and I had nothing to hide behind. I believed that I was a fair hand at giving advice to adults, but I wasn't so sure with kids.

While I thought it over, we could both hear Mungus above us, groaning his way through a series of situps. He had decided to join a health club so he could get in shape, but he wanted to get in shape first, so that nobody at the health club would deride him for not being in shape.

"Look," I finally said to Cindy. "You go to high school?"

"Newburyport High," she said.

"And the teachers, are they pretty good?"

"They're okay."

"Well, I want you to be a good teacher, too," I said.

"Huh?"

"We're all teachers," I said. "You're a teacher, I'm a teacher. And it's a simple rule of life that we teach people how to treat us."

"We do?"

"Yes, we do. If Glenn hits you and you forgive him

and he hits you again and you forgive him again, then you've taught him that hitting you is okay, and that he gets forgiven for it."

"Really?"

"Yes, really. If you hit him back or leave him, then you've taught him that hitting you is not okay."

"So I should hit him back?"

"No," I said. "You have to leave him."

"Really?"

"Really," I said. "If you don't leave him, then how will he learn that hitting you is not okay?"

"But I love him."

"No," I said, perhaps too strongly. "You can love him if he decides to stop hitting you. But you can't love someone who thinks it's okay to hit you, because if you do, then you're not loving yourself. If you love someone else, but don't love yourself, then it's not worth it."

"I read that in *Seventeen* once," Cindy said. She seemed to be impressed by the fact that I, apparently, subscribed to the magazine.

Of course there was nothing new in all of this. I had said it all to Molly many times when she was flailing herself over some rejection or other. And there had been times when I could see my marriage drifting over the edge and blamed myself, that Molly had said these things to me. "Putting out a shingle," we called it. The big difference was that Molly made quite a nice living at it.

"I understand," Cindy said. "I really do."

"And you can't hit yourself," I said.

"Hit myself? I never hit myself," she said.

"I don't mean with the hands. With the mind," I said.

"The mind?"

"It's called feeling guilty," I explained. "Don't spend a lot of time feeling guilty about leaving Glenn."

We went along in that vein for quite a while. The advice had been given, but Cindy's need to talk had not yet been filled. It would be a lot easier to do this stuff in a newspaper column, I thought. I could say it once, keep it short, and reach millions of people at a time.

After a second cup of tea Cindy admitted that maybe she didn't love Glenn as much as she thought, because she'd been thinking lately that if she broke off with him, maybe this kid David, who was cuter than Luke Perry, would ask her out.

"Cindy," I said, "people who ask for advice almost always know what they want the advice to be. They know what they need to do. What they are really looking for is the strength to do it."

Cindy thanked me. I told her to lace up her sneakers so she wouldn't trip on the way home. She gave me a long hug and then asked me a question that a lot of people had asked me.

"What's Oprah Winfrey like?" she said.

I hadn't the vaguest idea of what Oprah Winfrey was like. Off the air I had spent about twelve seconds with her.

"She's great," I said, "just great."

"Did you shake her hand when you met her?"

"Sure," I said.

Then Cindy put out a hand for me to shake. So she could tell her friends she had shaken the hand that shook the hand of Oprah.

At the door Cindy said, "I could tell just from watching you on TV that you were a really nice person."

For a long time I sat there, trying not to think about Noelle. I thought about Cindy and the boyfriend problems which, in her mind, probably loomed as large as the murders of Molly and Noelle did in mine. Why couldn't everything just be smaller? I wondered. Why couldn't it be that nothing was overwhelming? What I wanted most was to stay in this cozy little cottage and watch the spring turn to summer without my involvement. I wanted to walk away from Molly's murder just as I had walked away from her job. I wanted to find some nice safe little cases and write true crime books about them without getting my throat slashed, and I wanted to meet a woman and have kids, or at least get a dog and name him Mungus. But I knew it was all bullshit. I could no more walk away from Molly's murder than I could shed my own skin. So I would probably agonize and analyze and theorize until it wore me out or got me killed. Sometimes, I thought, choice is an illusion. We always end up doing what we have to do.

I went into my office and tore down the poster I had made of my worst book review. Then I called Joan and asked her to meet me.

"Should I get us a room?" she said.

"No," I said.

Joan didn't want to be seen in Boston. There was a doctor's convention in town. She said she would come to Newburyport.

That night at seven o'clock I met Joan at the old-fashioned soda fountain in Fowles, a favorite Newburyport hangout for Mungus and me. Fowles was a great place to meet someone because the store carried every magazine in creation and if your date was late, you could browse through magazine racks, which is my idea of a good time. But Joan wasn't late. She came breezing in like a prom queen, having no idea that I was about to clobber her.

We went outside and walked along the cobble-stone

streets. Like a tour guide I explained that all the redbrick buildings had gone up after the great fire of 1811.

"I made videotapes of all your TV appearances," Joan said after I gave her the short version of Newburyport's history. "It was awful about that woman. I wonder what they'll do now."

"I don't know," I said. I didn't want to tell Joan that I had been offered the job and had turned it down. That would have been a distraction from the real reason I had called her.

I took Joan's hand and we walked down to the Merrimack River. We strolled along the wharf. How many other strolling lovers are not really free to be together? I wondered. For a few minutes we were circled by gulls that thought we might be bread throwers. Joan searched through her purse, hoping that she had a piece of candy or something to throw to them. But she had nothing, and soon the gulls gave up in disgust.

I had come to love Joan during our time together. But I had come to love myself, too, and that's why we had to say goodbye.

"I've been thinking about your husband," I said.

"My husband?"

"Yes. He doesn't beat you, does he?"

"Goodness, no," she said.

"And he's never really been cruel to you."

"No," Joan said. The spring weather had brought out the locals, and the opening of the small shops in Market Square had lured tourists, so there were many people walking by the river. I was hoping that somebody would recognize me from TV, and ask for my autograph, but nobody did.

"Do you think he still loves you?" I said.

"Yes," she said. "I guess, in his own way."

"But he's just sort of caught up in making a living, and he's forgotten some important things, and he ignores you."

"Right," Joan said. She squeezed my hand tighter. I guess she could see what I was getting to.

"And you're . . . seeing me," I said.

Joan said nothing.

"I think you should try to work things out with him," I said.

"Oh."

"I think I'm not good for you, Joan. I'm not being fair to you. I'm keeping you from doing what you really need to do."

"You don't want to see me anymore?"

"That's not it, exactly. I don't want you to see me anymore. All it's doing is delaying what you need to do with your life."

I guess I had imagined a weepy goodbye, Joan rushing stiffly to her car. But it wasn't like that. We sat on one of the benches by the river and Joan cried with me a bit, then we went to Michael's Harborside restaurant. I had a great dinner, but Joan hardly touched her meal.

As we walked back to Joan's car she tried to make a comeback. "I think I could work on my marriage and we could still see each other," she said. "I just have to separate them in my mind. I mean, we've always had such good times together."

"I don't think it would work," I said coldly.

When Joan kissed me goodbye in the small downtown lot where she had parked, she held back nothing, including her tongue. It was a fiery kiss, and if it was her attempt to get me back, it almost worked. But I knew that if I stepped back now from this small nobility, I might never find the strength again.

Joan got into her car and rolled down the window.

"What happened?" she said.

"A girl came to the cottage this afternoon, looking for advice," I said.

"Boy problems?"

"Yes."

"I know how she feels," Joan said.

"She said that she could tell I was a nice person," I said.

Joan smiled. "I could have told you that, Scotty."

"Thanks."

"I think this advice thing has really changed you," Joan said. "You're more . . . I don't know, introspective. Is that the right word?"

"I guess. It means I'm looking inside myself," I said. I smiled. "Molly used to say that, remember? Look inside yourself."

"Yes," Joan said. "She said you could always find the answers inside yourself. What did you find, Scotty?"

"A certain amount of corruption," I said.

"Corruption?"

"The first time we made love, did it surprise you that I would have an affair with a married woman?"

"No," Joan said. "I knew you could be seduced."

"Yeah, that's me," I said with a grin. "Highly seducible."

And then something terrible hit me.

"Scotty, what's wrong?" Joan said. Her voice sounded distant. I knew I had a stunned look on my face. "Are you okay?"

"No, I'm not okay," I said, rushing from her. "But I think I know who murdered Molly."

CHAPTER 19

Some things are best done in the light. So it was ten o'clock the following morning when I drove down to Rockport to see my friend Crash Galovitch. It was in that picturesque town of painters and tourists that Crash lived, in the marina, on a forty-foot sailing ketch by the name of *Snake Eyes*.

The boatmaster directed me to Crash's slip. I found Crash on the deck of *Snake Eyes*, gutting fish on a wooden crate with a heavy duty fish knife.

"Permission to come aboard," I called, because that's what they always say in the movies.

"Hey, Scotty," Crash said, waving to me with the hand that held the knife. Its gleaming blade sparkled at me in the sunlight. Suddenly I didn't want to go aboard.

"Jesus, put that thing down," I said. "Those things scare the shit out of me."

"Oh." Crash laughed. He placed the knife on the crate and stood to greet me as I pulled myself onto the boat. "How they hanging, pal?" he said, offering me a hand that smelled of dead fish.

Crash seemed happy to see me. "Coffee?" he asked.

"Sure," I said. He stepped down into the cabin. I heard him banging around in the narrow galley, and a few minutes later he returned with coffee for both of us in tiny tin cups like the ones they give you in the state penitentiary.

"Well?" he said, handing me the coffee.

"Well?" I said.

"Come on, Scotty. Don't tease me. Did Dracut offer you the job?"

"He offered it," I said.

"All right!" Crash said. "This is great news, great news." Then he stopped. "You took it, of course?" he said.

I smiled. "Yeah, Crash, I took it. I'd have been crazy to turn it down."

Crash was ecstatic, and he wanted to celebrate. He ran over to the diner next to the marina to get us sandwiches. When he came back, he was all smiles and there was an extra spring in his step. "I stopped at the package store, too," he said. "Got some beer. And for you"—he waved a big paper bag at me—"wine coolers!" That was Crash, always remembering what people liked, and doing the thoughtful little thing.

After he put his food down in the ice chest, he came back on deck and cranked up *Snake Eyes* engine.

"We going sailing?" I asked.

"Nah, no wind. Let's just putter out a few miles and anchor. Have a few beers, shoot the shit."

I went down below and strapped on a life jacket. I had fallen off the deck one time in Miami.

I came up and stood behind the helm and watched Crash guide the sailboat, without its sails, out into the harbor. As the vista of ocean and deep blue sky widened around me, it all seemed so bountiful, so unconcerned with the matters that were everything to me. Did Noelle like the ocean? I wondered. Did Molly ever sail?

"Why so glum looking?" I heard Crash say. "You sure don't look like a guy who just signed on to become a highly paid international celebrity."

"I know who killed Molly," I said.

There was a long silence. Crash held the wheel and stared straight ahead. "What?" he finally said. "You can't be serious. You're not saying she was really murdered."

"She was."

"But who?"

"Lillian Gilmartin," I said.

"Oh, Scotty. That can't be. Lillian?"

Crash looped a length of line over the wheel and locked it in place while the boat moved forward. Then he swung around to give me all of his attention.

"All along I've been thinking that Molly's murder had something to do with her leaving the *Patriot*," I said. "But that's not it, not exactly."

"No?"

"She wasn't killed because she was leaving. She was killed because of where she was going?"

"What do you mean?"

"Molly loved Boston," I said. "She would never have taken her column to San Francisco or Washington. She was going to the *Boston Times*."

"Holy shit!" Crash said. "She was going to push Lillian out of her job?"

"For a second time," I said. "And it would be the third time Lillian got pushed out. When I interviewed Lillian, she told me that she lost her first advice column years ago when 'Dear Abby' and Ann Landers came on the scene. Lillian called them 'the nitwit sisters.' She was practically psycho on the subject. Now, here was Molly doing it to her again."

"God," Crash said. "I can't believe it."

"Believe it," I said. "She's very unstable. The way I figure it, she must have called Molly and asked her to meet for a drink, you know, a bury-the-hatchet kind of thing. She knew where Molly lived. She probably chose someplace that was close so Molly would walk, but someplace where Molly would have to cross Huntington Avenue. She tried to run Molly over, but she missed. She probably called Molly later and apologized for standing her up, said she got tied up or something, then probably asked her to meet the next night, same time, same place. That night she didn't miss."

"Jesus," Crash said. "Then Lillian must have killed Noelle when she found out Noelle was being set up to get the job Lillian wanted."

"Right."

"What about you?" he said, his eyes glancing madly about. "Are you in danger?"

"I don't think so," I said. "I've already got the job. Killing me wouldn't help. Besides, Lillian's still got her job at the *Times*."

"Maybe," Crash said. "But you'd better watch your back."

For a long time we moved along the coast, a few miles offshore. We talked about whether or not to turn Lillian over to the police. Crash was against it. "There's no evidence," he said. "It won't get you anywhere. It will just steal the spotlight from you. Everybody will run the murder story instead of the 'male advice columnist' story. You'll be a footnote."

"You're probably right," I said.

"Just let her be," Crash urged. "Sooner or later she'll

pay for what she's done. They always do. You have to put all this behind you now and think about yourself. You got the job. Congratulations."

"Thanks," I said. "And congratulations to you."

"To me?"

"Sure," I said. "Don't be so modest. Dracut told me the contest was your idea."

I was lying. After I had left Joan the previous night, I had gone home to the cottage and replayed my taped interview with Dracut. I wanted to find out if I had asked him whose idea the contest was. I hadn't, and he hadn't mentioned it.

"Really? He told you?" Crash said. "I thought for sure he'd take all the credit."

We chugged along for another fifteen minutes, then Crash put down the anchor in sight of a pair of small islands. In the distance I could see other sailboats, their sails sagging in the still air. Crash broke out the beer and sandwiches, and the wine coolers for me.

We unfolded a pair of deck chairs and lugged them over to starboard, where we made ourselves comfortable and propped our feet up on the lifeline that ran, about waist high, the length of the boat. Just two guys getting away from it all on a sunny morning. While we ate and drank, the boat swayed gently back and forth, and we talked about the old days down in Miami Beach. One time when Crash's wife was away we had gotten a couple of very pretty young women on the boat and told them we were the owner and publisher of *Vogue* magazine. That day things had gone as well as they can go when you get two females on a boat. Now Crash and I laughed about that. We talked about the fact that Crash didn't seem to be as much as a skirt chaser these days. He seemed more interested in gambling, the vice that had gotten him in six miles deep with the bookies.

Finally I said to him, "Look, Crash, how much do you want?"

"Huh?"

"The kickback," I said. "How much did you have in mind?"

He didn't answer, just stared out at the sea, sipping from his beer can.

"Crash, don't be embarrassed about it," I said. "This is Scotty talking. We go way back, remember. I'm not blind. I know you helped me win this Molly thing. I don't know who you bribed or threatened and I don't want to know, but I know you rigged it. And let's face it, Crash, we might be friends, but you didn't go to all this bother for purely altruistic reasons."

Crash laughed. "You had it figured out all along, huh?" Crash said. Now he gave me a big smile. "Good man."

He took a big swig of his beer. "Look," he said, "I'm not asking for a big cut. I'm not the kind of guy that would gouge you."

"I know that," I said. "How much?"

"Well," he said. Now he pulled his feet down from the lifeline and sat up in the deck chair, as if to add an air of dignity to the closing of the deal. "The way I got it figured, it will take you a few years to get into the really big bucks, you know. But I figure this year you ought to clear three hundred grand. I was thinking, well, I got it all figured out. Ten grand a month would keep the goons off my back until I'm all paid up. All they got to see is that I'm making payments and keeping up with the interest. So I get them taken care of. Then next year we see how

you're doing. I was thinking maybe twenty percent.
How's that sound?"

"Sounds fair to me," I said.

"Shake on it," Crash said. He gave me his hand.

"Okay, we got a deal," Crash said. "Now, I got to tell
you something, because you'll find out sooner or later.
Don't get mad at me, okay?"

"Okay."

"The truth is I didn't give you as much help as I
wanted to. I figured for sure Dracut would put me on the
selection committee, seeing as how the contest was my
idea, but he wouldn't do it. Said I was going to be
squiring the contestants all over the country on the
publicity tour, maybe even fucking them, and it wouldn't
look good me being on the committee. So all I could do
was get you in the semifinals, give you the chance to
write some letters and show your stuff, then I was cut out
of the loop. You did the rest on your own. But hell, that's
worth twenty percent, ain't it."

"Sure," I said. "Worth every penny." Inside I was
raging. This miserable son of a bitch had killed my
Molly. And he had killed Noelle. I wanted to just drop
him in the ocean and be done with it. But it was too soon
to play my hand.

"Why me?" I said. "Crash, why did you bet on me?"

I already knew the answer, of course. I had realized it
when I was saying goodbye to Joan, when I had finally
looked for answers inside myself, instead of everybody
else.

"Are you kidding?" Crash said. "You were perfect."

"Perfect?"

"Sure. When Dracut told me to go ahead with the
contest, I thought Christmas had come early. Hell, you
were always wise, even back in Florida when I first met

you, you always had good common sense. You used to give me advice all the time. On top of that, you have the writing talent. You were a friend of Molly's, you already lived in Massachusetts. And best of all, you were corruptible."

"Corruptible?" I said. "That's how you think of me?"

"Certainly," he said, as if he had paid me a fine compliment. "Hell, that's how we got together in the first place, you writing puff pieces for my clients."

"Right," I said. I guess I'd been hoping that Crash would say something different, something that would prove me wrong, something that would show that my character had not been a factor in the whole tragic equation. But no such luck.

For a full five minutes I was as silent as a stone. How do you play this scene, Scotty? I wondered. I knew that the sea didn't care what I did, and there were terrible things that I could get away with. The boats in the distance were much too far away to know a push from a fall. But I wouldn't do it. I wasn't going to strangle Crash Galovitch with my bare hands, I wasn't going to knock him into the water. I wasn't even going to push him. Hell, I could accidentally knock him out, and then how would I get back to shore? As immense as his crimes were, there was nothing dramatic or violent to be done, except to just say it out loud.

"Lillian Gilmartin didn't kill Molly," I said.

Crash looked at me. "But you said—"

"I lied," I said. "I made it up."

"Why?"

"So you would feel secure," I said. "So you would be sure you had gotten away with it. So you would confirm what I knew. Lillian didn't kill Molly. You killed her, Crash."

"Me?" Now Crash placed his beer can on the deck and turned to face me in his chair. I could see that his arms and legs were stiffened for battle.

"You killed my best friend, you son of a bitch," I said. "You killed her and you tried to rig the contest for me. And you did it all for money, didn't you? You couldn't even let Molly have her life because she'd still be 'Dear Molly' someplace, and your patsy wouldn't make enough money to pay his kickbacks. And when you saw that Dracut was going to give the job to his girlfriend instead of me, you killed her, too. Jesus, Crash, how could you do such an immoral thing?"

"Look, Scotty, just put all this crazy shit out of your mind, okay. It will just drive you insane. We've got a good thing going now. You've got the job."

"I didn't take it," I said.

"What?"

"I didn't take it. I turned it down."

"Unfucking believable!" Crash roared. "You have to take that job. I need the money." He bolted out of his chair. I thought he was going to lunge for me. Instead, he knocked his chair aside and walked silently back to the helm. He stared at the wheel for a moment, then, bristling with anger, he paced back and forth across the narrow deck. I stared out at the restless water. So, I thought, this is what it's like when you accuse somebody of murder. You say it, and then you both sulk like squabbling lovers. It was an absurd situation, but now we would have to come up with conversation for the trip back to the marina. We both knew that Crash was in no danger of going to jail. There wasn't a speck of evidence against him, just the knowledge we shared.

"I want you to take the job," I heard Crash say a few minutes later. His voice was cold and controlled. I stood and turned. Crash was coming slowly toward me. The fish knife was in his hand.

"Jesus," I said.

"There's something you have to understand, Scotty," he said as he moved closer. "If you don't take the job, I will come after you and I will cut you open with this knife. I can do it, easily. That sort of thing doesn't bother me. I don't know why, but it doesn't. I know Molly was your friend and I'm sorry about that, but to tell you the truth I didn't feel anything when I killed her. It was like running over a toy doll, no different. I looked it up in a book. I'm a sociopath. You know what that is? It means I have no conscience."

When Crash was two feet from me, he stopped and looked into my eyes, asking for my answer. He twisted the knife back and forth in his hand. I was petrified. The glimmering of that awful blade brought me back to that night with Fred McHale, and suddenly I could feel again the searing pain as McHale's blade cut into my neck. I was afraid of the blade more than anything, and Crash knew it. Though the serrated blade on Crash's knife was smaller than McHale's had been, it was now as frightening as the jaws of a shark.

"Please," I said. It was the same pitiful word I said to Fred McHale when he had brought the knife to my throat, and I knew I would die.

"Just take the job, Scotty."

I thought in that moment about Noelle. She must have known she was going to die when Crash grabbed her on the back stairs of that hotel in Miami. He must have had a weapon, maybe even this knife that now held me in place. She must have fought him, she must have tried ferociously to scratch at his eyes, to kick him, to claw him. It must have been an awful battle, and as Crash got more and more control of her small body, there must have been a moment when Noelle wanted to give up, a moment when she thought she could just go over the edge and grab a railing on the way down. She must have started to think that the cold brick stairwell offered some slim hope and the knife offered none. If I had been there, I could have told her: there are no railings on the way down.

Again the blade glistened. "Are you going to do what I tell you, Scotty?" Crash said. I remembered the helplessness I felt the night that Molly had died and how I conned myself into thinking that I could have done something about it. If only I had been in the right place at the right time, I had thought then. But I wasn't. In the months that had passed since Molly's death, I had learned that it wasn't my fault. Sometimes there was just nothing to be done.

But now there is this moment, I heard Molly say in my mind. And you can do something.

Suddenly I felt a surge of energy in my feet. I sprang toward Crash. He lunged forward with the knife as I came at him. "Damn you!" he screamed. The blade caught me in the shoulder, then glanced away. I went into a crouch and I felt Crash's arm come down on my back. The wind went out of me. Then I slammed my head up into his jaw. He pitched back slightly, and I went after the hand that held the knife. He threw up his knee, ramming my thigh and just missing the spot that would have put this battle to an end. I yanked him toward me, and our combined momentum threw us against the lifeline. I twisted the hand that held the knife, but Crash would not let go. It came closer and closer to me, as the boat pitched back and forth. I held his wrist high and rammed my head into Crash's chest. He smelled of sweat and fish.

There was a sickening sound of ribs cracking, but still Crash held his knife. There was no expression in his eyes, and every move he made was aimed at putting that knife to my throat. We were equally matched, so we struggled for a long time, each of us sweating and breathless, no one getting the upper hand. But I knew that I would lose a tie game. If we both ran out of steam, he would still have the knife.

But I've got the life jacket, I thought, and I knew the sea would be kinder to me than to him.

I held back the knife with all my might and lifted one leg over the lifeline, then the other. Now, on the other side, I put one hand on that tight cable that was supposed to save lives, and held Crash's wrist with the other. I dug my feet into the taffrail and leaned back, letting my weight do the work of pulling Crash forward. He lost his balance. I twisted the knife out of his hand and watched it fall into the water. But the fight was not gone from Crash Galovitch. He still struggled. "It's not too late, Scotty!" he shouted, as if I were miles away. "We can both be rich." With all the strength left in my arm I pulled myself up toward him and wrapped my arms around his body. Then I leaned back and let us fall. Crash spilled over the lifeline on top of me, and we crashed into the cold Atlantic water.

I would have saved his life, I suppose. But I didn't get the chance. Crash floundered about in the water for a few seconds, trying to get his bearings. He looked at the boat, as if he would try to board it again. But I guess he knew he could never win a battle in the water with a man who wore a life jacket. He began to swim desperately toward the islands, much faster than I could move, with the life jacket holding me straight up and bobbing in the water. I knew he wouldn't make it. It was much too far. I watched him for a while, shrinking in the distance like my wife's car on that rainy afternoon that now seemed years ago. Just before he disappeared there was a wildness in his movements and I could hear him shrieking something. He went under. Then there was a brief flash of color on the flat water as he emerged once. And then he was gone.

I was in the water for two hours before a real estate consultant from Nantucket picked me up in his sloop. Then there were the police and the Coast Guard to deal with, and it turned into a very long day.

When I got back to Plum Island, the cottage was dark. Mungus had left a note. He was spending the night with a woman named Gloria, whom I had never heard of. Just as well, I thought, I'm not up to telling my story. By midnight I was in bed beneath my slanted ceiling. I had my windows open so I could listen to the music of the ocean, but tonight it was not music, and instead of putting me to sleep, it kept me awake. I was finally dozing off, though, when I heard sounds. Footsteps. There was somebody downstairs in the dark.

I climbed out of bed and walked to the top of the stairs. "Mungus?" I called out, "Is that you?" figuring maybe his lady love had learned earlier than the last one that Mungus is not an ambitious person and had tossed him out of bed.

There was no answer, but I was sure that somebody had walked through the front door and now was standing in the dark of our wooden cottage. It made me angry. I wanted it to be Fred McHale so that I could go down there and pound the shit out of him. But Fred McHale, like Molly, was gone, and there was nothing to be done about it.

"Who's there?" I called. I was frightened but unwilling

simply to hide in my bed and let some home-invasion specialist walk off with the VCR. Still in my pajamas, I went to my closet and fumbled around for my Smith & Wesson.

"Who's there?" I called again. "Cindy?" I called, thinking perhaps my young friend had fought with her family and had come to me for shelter.

With gun in hand I crept slowly down the stairs. This is crazy I thought, the invader could have a gun just as easily as I could. But I saw no other choice. You either hide from things or you face them. At the bottom of the stairs I stood quietly for a long time. I was beginning to believe that I had heard nothing more than the settling of the cottage at night, when somebody jumped me from behind and knocked me to the floor. The gun flew out of my hand and landed with a thud somewhere in the dark.

It was a man, I could see, not particularly big, and after he knocked me down, he dashed for the door. Instead of letting him go, I reached out and grabbed his foot and yanked him down with me. He started swinging at me in the dark. I hit back and felt my fist make contact with something and he let out a groan. Who the hell is this, I wondered, somebody who didn't like the advice I gave him? Then I grabbed his shoulders with two hands and pinned him to the floor. By now I was pretty sure that he didn't have a weapon. I straddled his chest and slapped him silly the way my brother used to do to me whenever I called him "flat nose." I put up an arm to ward off the fists I thought would be aimed at my face. But there were none. I felt the man give up. With my knees clamped round his chest like a vice I edged us both over to the table by the couch. I reached up and turned on the lamp.

In the light I found myself looking down at a man I had never met. He was about my age, maybe a little older, with thinning hair, a round face, and he wore eyeglasses, which, miraculously, had not fallen off in the scuffle. He didn't look like a burglar. He looked up at me sheepishly.

"Who the hell are you?" I said.

"Jim Bentley," he said.

"Jim who?"

"Joan's husband," he explained.

"Oh, Christ," I said. Suddenly I was the invader. I loosened my grip on him and rolled off him.

"Then you know," I said. He had broken into my house and attacked me, but still I was embarrassed.

Jim Bentley sat up and leaned against the couch while we both caught our breath. He buttoned his white shirt and wiped the lenses of his glasses with a tissue from his pocket.

"I've known for a long time," he said. "I followed you to a motel once. Then I followed you home."

He sat up straight. I stared at his eyes and he stared at mine, each of us checking to see if the other was about to strike again. After a moment we leaned back against the couch and stretched our legs out, an unspoken agreement that the fight was over. In the strange way that men bond, we had been brought together by fighting physically, and now we were just two guys talking it out.

"And you took a shot at me," I said.

"Yes," he said proudly. "But I wasn't trying to hit you, just scare you off. I thought you'd suspect me and you'd stop seeing Joan."

"But it didn't work that way," I said. "Why didn't you try again?"

"When I got home that night and realized I could have killed somebody, I fell apart," he said. "I started shaking. I'm a doctor. I'm supposed to save lives, not take them.

I decided I'd better just ignore the affair. I thought Joan would come to her senses and I'd have her back."

"So what's this attack tonight about? Or were you just in the neighborhood?"

"Joan told me about the affair last night," he said.

"Did she tell you it's over?"

"Yes," he said.

"Then why?"

"Now that she knew that I knew, I couldn't ignore it," he said. "I had to do something. You know how it is, being a man and all, you've got to stand up for your honor and all that."

"So you figured you'd drive up to Plum Island and kill me?"

"Oh, goodness, no," Jim Bentley said. "I didn't even bring a gun. I didn't know what I'd do exactly. Maybe take a poke at you. Or steal something. Or vandalize the house. I didn't know. Didn't that ever happen to you, where you know you've got to do something, but you don't know exactly what?"

"Yes," I said. "I guess it has. But I came down those stairs with a gun. You could have gotten yourself killed. You must love Joan quite a lot."

"I do," he said. "Don't you?"

"Yes," I said.

"But not enough to fight for her?" he said. "Is that it?"

I had to give his question some thought, and I realized he was wrong. I did love Joan. But I didn't think I could show that love by breaking up her marriage, wrecking her relationship with her kid, and asking her to turn in her credit cards and start clipping coupons.

"I guess you're right," I said to Jim Bentley.

I called Joan and woke her up. I told her what was going on and asked her to drive up to Plum Island to hash things out. Then I changed into some clothes and put on some coffee. It was going to be a long night after a long day. Jim and I bonded some more, in less violent ways, while we waited for Joan. He didn't mean to neglect the family, he said, he just wanted to make a good living for them.

"That's how I was brought up," he said. "A man works hard to make a living for his family."

"Look," I said, "you're a doctor, right? If you just work a normal forty-hour week, you make more than most people need to live on."

"I guess," he said.

"So the rest of the money you make for all those extra hours is really no more than green pieces of paper," I said.

"Huh?"

"Green pieces of paper. You put them on the bottom of your stack. But your stack is so big that you are never going to get to them, which means they are worthless."

"I never thought of it that way," he said.

"Well, you should. All those hours that you could spend with your wife and your son, you're trading away for green pieces of paper that you will never spend. You know, when you're through collecting green pieces of paper for the bottom of your pile, you can't use them to buy back the years you could have had with Joan and the kid. Those years will be gone forever, and all the green pieces of paper in the world won't bring them back."

When Joan arrived she was as embarrassed as I had been, but before long we were all friends. We sat at the rickety wooden table in the kitchen and drank coffee. I gave them my best advice on how to keep their marriage from failing like mine. We stayed up all night, going over their past joys and past hurts. It was a ridiculous situation. It was a tense situation, too, and at one point Jim and I got into a fistfight and he bloodied my nose. But things did calm down, and among the three of us we got their marriage pretty well worked out, and at sunrise they left, vowing to work at it.

It was a bright morning, and cool, so I put on a sweater, poured myself some more coffee, and walked over to the beach. It had been less than twenty-four hours since Crash Galovitch went under, but already the ocean was something I could love again. The Molly case was over, but now there was a little thing called my life to be dealt with.

Dear Molly, I thought, *I'm a middle-aged man who has no lady, no money, and no job. I feel as if I'm starting over and I'm scared. Do I keep on writing magazine articles and hope for the best? Or do I actually make the rounds of employment agencies and look for a nine to five? Both choices make me want to throw up. What should I do? Signed, Baffled in Boston.*

Dear Baffled, I heard Molly say in my mind, *Don't be such a schmuck. Freelancing is a young man's game and you're much too old for an entry-level position. Find what you are meant to do, and do it. Love, Molly.*

I figured Lawrence Dracut was the kind of guy who got into the office early. So at eight o'clock I left my spot by the ocean and walked back to the cottage and called him.

"Mr. Scotland," he said, "I've been expecting this call."

"You have?"

"Sure," he said. "You've changed your mind. You want the 'Dear Molly' job. Though I guess we'll have to call it Dear Scotty, or some such thing."

"Yes," I said. "If it's still available."

"The job is yours," he said. "I knew you'd come around."

"How did you know?" I said.

"Because you are a person who likes to take care of people," he said. "It's your nature, and this is the perfect job for that."

"Well, I haven't acted like much of a caretaker in the last couple of years," I said.

"Perhaps," he said. "Human action can be modified to some extent, but human nature cannot be changed."

"Lawrence Dracut?" I asked.

"Oh, no." He laughed. "Abraham Lincoln."

After I hung up I went back and stood by the ocean. *Dear Molly,* I thought, *This is going to be a hoot. Me, as an advice columnist. Me, with a real job. And Mungus as my stooge. It will be fun, and maybe from time to time I can do some good. And Molly,* I thought, *if sometimes the road gets a little dark and I am the one who needs help, who feels insecure, who needs to magically draw wisdom from the air, that's okay, too. Because with you around I'll always know I have a friend I can turn to for advice. Love, Scotty.*

MURDER & MYSTERY

BERKLEY
PRIME
CRIME

__NORTH STAR CONSPIRACY
by Miriam Grace Monfredo
0-425-14720-7/$4.99

When a freed slave dies in 1854 New York, a suspicious Underground Railroad supporter raises her doubts about the death—and about so-called sympathizers.
__Also by Miriam Grace Monfredo: SENECA FALLS INHERITANCE 0-425-14465-8/$4.99

__MURDER IN BRIEF by Carroll Lachnit
0-425-14790-8/$4.99

When ex-cop Hannah Barlow goes to law school and her moot-court partner is killed, Hannah must decipher a complex case of mistaken identities, blackmail, and murder.

__THE BOY'S TALE by Margaret Frazer
0-425-14899-8/$4.99

When the half-brothers of King Henry VI receive death threats, Sister Frevisse offers them safety. But even a nunnery is no sanctuary from the ambitious and the wicked.
__Also by Margaret Frazer: THE BISHOP'S TALE 0-425-14492-5/$4.50

__GOING NOWHERE FAST by Gar Anthony Haywood
0-425-15051-8/$4.99

En route to the Grand Canyon, retired cop Joe Loudermilk and his wife find a dead man in their trailer. Soon they are crossing the desert in search of the killer—with the FBI, the National Park Service, the L.A. Raiders, and the Mob on their heels.